CAPTURING JASMINA

India's Street Kids: Book 1

Capturing Jasmina

KIMBERLY RAE

journey**forth**®

Greenville, South Carolina

Library of Congress Cataloging-in Publication Data
Rae, Kimberly.
    Capturing Jasmina / Kimberly Rae.
        pages cm
        Summary: "Jasmina, a young girl in India, and her brother,
Samir, are sold by their father to a man promising them a better life.
They soon discover they are actually child slaves in a sweatshop"—
Provided by publisher.
        ISBN 978-1-60682-853-3 (perfect bound pbk.) — ISBN 978-
1-60682-855-7 (ebook) [1. Human trafficking—Fiction. 2. Street
children—Fiction. 3. India—Fiction.] I. Title.
        PZ7.R1231Cap 2014
        [Fic]—dc23
                                                            2013049039

Cover Photo: iStockphoto.com © vijaya_5712

Design by Nathan Hutcheon
Page layout by Michael Boone

© 2014 by BJU Press
Greenville, South Carolina 29614
JourneyForth Books is a division of BJU Press

Printed in the United States of America

ISBN 978-1-60682-853-3
eISBN 978-1-60682-855-7

15 14 13 12 11 10 9 8 7 6 5 4 3 2 1

For the Street Kids

Ye shall not afflict any widow, or fatherless child.
If thou afflict them in any wise,
and they cry at all unto me,
I will surely hear their cry.

Exodus 22:22–23

contents

Prologue

He sold me. I still cannot decide whether my father was fully aware of his choice when he traded me for money. Did he really believe the man would give me free education and a future job, a life better than the poverty we had always known? Or could he sense the man's lies, see the anticipation in how his hands shook as they held out the wad of bills?

My mother did; I am certain of that. My memories show me her narrowed eyes and the worry that creased her forehead, and I remember the way she braved breaking into their conversation and stating boldly that I should stay.

The memories of my father are clear as well. How can I forget them? That day is imprinted in my mind and cannot be erased any more than ink can be removed once it has soaked into paper—however unwanted the words may be. Had I not been so foolishly hopeful, I would have seen through my own pretense and known the truth.

My dreams are clearer than I allow my thoughts to be. In my dreams I see my father glance up at the taller, well-dressed man. I see questions in his eyes, questions that must have been answered because his hand reaches out for the money, the "deposit" of my supposed future earnings from a rich foreign sponsor. My father's hands do not shake as the other man's did. In the faded pictures of my nightmares, he then turns to me and says, "I never wanted you."

If I wake up screaming or crying, I clamp my hand over my mouth or cover my face with my sheet, not wanting to admit even to myself that a dream could affect me so. I swallow hard, use the sheet to wipe my sweat-drenched face, and force myself to open my eyes. But all I see is darkness. Darkness whether my eyes are open or closed.

I lie down again and remember watching from the cooking area behind the flimsy bamboo door, dropping a spoon into the metal pot I held so he would hear the clanging noise and know I was there. He would know I heard every word as he bartered my life away.

Not once did he look at me. He looked at my mother when he refused her plea that I remain at home. He looked at the man again when he promised that Samir and I would provide my mother and him a better future.

And that is where my memories blur into confusion. The rejection of my father selling me, though painful, is not that surprising considering our poverty and my lack of worth as a female. What I cannot understand is why he also sold Samir, his son. Everyone knows it is a blessing from the gods to have a son. A daughter will marry and leave the family, providing no benefit; a son, however, is forever responsible to care for his parents and thus insures lifelong security.

Why would my father give that up for the temporary benefit of a few hundred rupees? Our family was poor, but no poorer than our neighbors. We were often hungry, but not to the point of starvation. We lived in a one-room bamboo shack, but my father's fishing business, even when it did not provide income, still at least provided a few fish to eat.

It has proven impossible to forget Samir's face the moment Father told him to go with the man. On it was fear, anger, betrayal. From the time he was a toddler, Samir had gleefully utilized his position of superiority over me. It did not matter that I was older. He was the son. Though at times I was certain I hated him, seeing him go from arrogant and even cruel to lost and afraid hurt something deep inside me.

I suppose his hurt ran deep through me because it matched my own. Though he had been favored, pampered, and nearly worshipped, we both were betrayed.

Why?

If I ever find my parents, that is the one question I will ask. Why? Why was a small bundle of money worth more than family? Why were we so little valued as to be considered disposable?

Much time has passed since that day. I hope to go back to our little hut near the sea to find our parents, but until now I have held back. I pretend I want to know, but the truth is I am a coward. I know as long as I have only questions, I am safe. Safe from answers that will break me, from truth that will destroy what little of my heart is left.

Asha says the truth will set you free. I have not told her yet that the truth can be the most enslaving thing of all.

Dear Samir,

Today the lady I'm staying with—her name is Asha—gave me this book full of blank pages. I asked her what kind of book it was, with no story, but she said it was for my story. She said I should write out what happened since you and I ~~left~~ were taken from home.

I asked her why. She said I should write it for me, so I could think through everything and sort the truth from the lies. She said I should also write it for you, so that ~~if~~ when I find you, everything will be in one place.

Because this is the first thing that has ever belonged to just me, I am going to be totally honest and write exactly how I think and feel. You will not like some of it, Samir, so later I will decide whether I will let you read it or only tell you the important parts. If you have learned to read by then, that is.

Auntie Asha—she said I could call her that—is older, probably at least twenty. She is dark like us, but she lived all her life in America. Her husband has white skin and yellow hair! He looks scary, but I like his smile. It is funny—the white man's Bangla is better than Asha's. He says that is because he grew up in India but Auntie Asha has been in India for only a few years.

I asked her why anyone would want to leave America, where everyone is rich, to come live here. She said God sent her. I asked, "Which god?"

"There is only one true God, the one who made everything."

She has some very strange ideas, but she is giving me a safe place to stay until I find you or our parents.

Are you still angry with them, Samir? I am trying to be, but it is hard to be angry when my heart is so filled up with ~~sadness hopelessness worry fear~~ other things.

In this book I will write the story of what happened. By the time all the pages are filled, hopefully I will have found you and our parents and we will all be together again.

Auntie Asha says she will pray to her God that He will work everything for good. I said, "Why not just pray for me to find my family? That would be good." She said that God works in mysterious ways.

Like I said, she is strange.

I have to go now. It is suppertime, and we are going to eat something other than rice! I think I will like living with these Americans. She is cooking something called pizza; it does not smell anything like curry. I will write later to tell you how it tastes.

Your sister,
Jasmina

one
The Beginning of My Story

My small brother, Samir, was what Americans call a big jerk. When we were younger, he used to laugh when I had to stay inside to do chores while he played with the other boys in the street. He would smirk while he and Father ate, knowing I was hiding just behind the door, waiting for my turn, a hand to my stomach to keep it from growling. He would eat until he was fat just so I would have less.

I found ways to have my revenge. One night I ground extra chilies into his curry sauce. It was so spicy he cried; then he wiped his eyes and the sauce on his fingers got chili spice in his eyes. I was punished for that, but it was worth it.

Life was pretty boring in our hut near the sea. For the first ten years of my existence, every day had the same routine. My father went out during the day to fish; my mother stayed home to clean our hut and prepare the meals. I liked the sound of the sea at night. I did not like having to do all the chores with Mother while my brother played.

"It's not fair," I used to say. "Why can't I go out and play too?"

"You are a girl" was all the answer I got. I learned quickly that being a girl was bad. It meant you got less food, less freedom, and less attention. My father would come home and ask my brother to sit with him and tell him about his day. I wished just once he would ask me.

"Father, do you want to know how my day went?" I once asked as I took his plate after supper.

"Why would I want to know that?" He laughed. "A woman's day cannot be interesting. Go get me more rice."

That night something began growing inside me. It was like darkness, but alive and strong. It made a hole inside me and then it grew. I changed from sad to angry.

When the man came to our house to speak with Father, I did not even look at him. Who cared what one man had to say to another?

But my mother looked ~~afraid~~ nervous. She stood outside the door and listened.

"What is it, Mother?"

She shook her head. "I do not know, but I do not trust this man. He is too well dressed."

Curious, I stood beside her and peeked through the cracks in the bamboo structure. "I will give them a good education, for free," the man said. "They will grow up to get good jobs and be able to take care of you." Father crossed his arms, and his eyebrows went together as they did when he was considering something.

"They will send home money each month, and you will be rich."

"Even the girl?" my father asked. I held my breath. What were they talking about?

The man nodded. My father nodded. I looked at my mother; she did not nod. Her mouth was one tight line. I gasped when she entered the room and the conversation.

"I need the girl at home with me, to help with the work."

"Don't be ridiculous." I saw my father wave away the words from my mother's mouth. "This man is offering free education."

"You said she didn't need an education."

I thought about the secret times, while Father was away, when my mother pulled down her one book and taught me to read by it. She offered to teach Samir too, but he refused. Father couldn't read, he said, so he didn't need to either. I knew it was just because he wanted to play instead of study. Samir always chose the easier path. I felt a sense of satisfaction that I could read but my brother, nearly nine years old, still could not.

Father spoke to Mother again. "This man also says she will have a sponsor, who will send us money every month."

"Money? Why?"

My father shrugged. "Who cares why? These foreigners have so much money they just give it away."

"I don't like it."

"Hush, woman. You know we can't afford a dowry for her to be married. This is an important opportunity."

My mother looked back to where I stood, hidden behind the bamboo. "What about our son?"

"Hmm." At this my father rubbed his chin in thought. "I want him to help me with the business."

"It has to be them both," the man said quickly, his words shooting out like the strike of a coiled snake. His voice had taken on a hard tone, but then he smiled and changed his voice back to light and friendly. "You would not want your daughter to have more education than your son, would you?"

My father hesitated. The man reached into the pocket of his expensive pants with no holes. "Just to prove to you that I am sincere, I will give you a deposit." He held out a handful of bills. My father's eyes grew huge.

I heard the man chuckle. "This is just the beginning," he said. "You don't want to miss out on such an opportunity, do you? But you must decide today. Right now."

That was the day my father chose to trade us for money. I have not seen my father or my mother since.

two
My First Day Away from Home

As we rode away in the mini taxi with three wheels, called an *auto*, Samir looked over at me, frowning. "What is happening? Where are we going? Who is this man?"

My brother had arrived home just as the man was walking out the door. My father called to Samir, pointing toward the auto. "This man will take you to get a good education. You will be able to get a better job and have a good life. Work hard, then come back to bring us into your good life too."

Then my father looked at me. "Bring honor to our family."

That was it? That was all he had to say to me? My heart plunged inside me. My stomach started to feel sick, probably because my heart had dropped down on it and was crushing it painfully.

Samir began asking questions, but the man gripped his shoulder and directed him toward the vehicle. I took one last look at my mother. Her eyes were wet like mine. "I will write to you from the school," I promised. I did not know it was a promise I would not be allowed to keep.

As we rode away and I answered Samir's questions—the ones that I could—I realized the man had never said the word *school* to my parents, nor had he given them any information about where he was taking us. He had not waited long enough for us to pack. Perhaps he knew we had nothing of value to bring.

That empty place inside me where anger lived began to fill with fear. What would happen to me? To my brother? My stomach felt even worse.

"Why didn't you talk them out of it?" Samir yelled. He reached across the seat and twisted my ear. "Why didn't you warn me so I could run away? I don't want to spend all day in school!"

I began to cry, which made him angry. He shoved me, then scooted as far over toward the opposite window as he could. After we rode for a long time, he stopped looking angry. I had stopped crying, not because I was no longer afraid but just because I was tired of crying. I was looking at the towns we passed by. How busy they were!

We rode for ~~an hour~~ ~~two hours~~ what felt like forever. I am not sure how long it took; I only know it was so long I stopped trying to memorize the way. Were I to jump from the auto and somehow escape, I could never find my way back home. We had come too far.

Samir looked over at me. "Where do you think we are going?" he asked. His superior face and tone were missing. At one time I would have thought it would make me feel better to see him afraid, but it didn't.

I had no answer but the truthful one. "I don't know."

three
Arriving at the Factory

When the auto finally stopped just outside a huge building made of brick, my curiosity nudged me out to get a better look. There was something very strange about this building. Strange in a way that knotted my insides.

"I don't think this is a school," Samir whispered beside me. "A school would not be so big, or so closed up."

So he too had noticed there were no windows.

I wanted to clutch his arm, anything to help push away this terrible feeling I had. I lightly touched his hand, but he jerked away. I sniffed, trying not to cry.

"Don't do that," he snarled.

"What?" I sniffed again.

"That sniffing thing you always do before you start crying. I hate it. It may work on Mother, but it won't work on me."

I sniffed again, and he pinched me. I bit my lip and looked around. Maybe if I thought of something else, I would not start crying. It would do no good to have Samir angry and sullen. I might need his help later once we started school.

If there was a school.

A loud sound suddenly bellowed out from somewhere nearby. I clamped my hands over my ears. "What is that?" I shouted.

"What?" Samir shouted back.

I could barely hear him over the sound. "What is that sound?"

Just then two wide double doors in the front of the building opened and people came pouring out. It reminded me of the time Samir stepped on an ant hill and the whole colony swarmed in every direction.

They rushed past us, around the auto. We were jostled and bumped, and I finally got back inside the auto just because it felt safer there.

As I watched I noticed something important. All the people running from the building were my size or smaller.

They were all children.

Finding Out the Truth

When the last child had disappeared from view, the man who had paid my father motioned for us to follow him. He started toward the building.

I did not follow. I felt frozen to my seat, kept still by fear and dread and confusion.

When he noticed I was not with him, he walked back to the auto and yanked me from it. He held me by the elbow, and I cried out in pain from his hard grip.

"If this is a school, why are none of the children wearing uniforms?"

The question had come from my mouth without my ~~thinking~~ consciously choosing to say it. The man dropped my arm. The relief I felt was short lived because he used his hand to slap me across the face. I stepped back and stared at him. Samir's eyes were huge, but he did not step forward to protect or defend me, but I ~~think~~ hope he may have wanted to.

"Don't ask me any questions." The man's voice had nothing of the friendliness he had used on my father. It was hard and cold. "I didn't bring you here to think."

Wasn't that what one was supposed to do at school? Think?

Another question was ready to burst out, but I kept it inside by biting both lips closed. The man grabbed my arm again and started dragging me toward the building. Samir followed.

We three entered the massive structure. I had to squint because without windows the building was very dark inside. When he flipped on a switch near the door, electric lights blinked on and I gasped.

The entire building was full. Row upon row of small tables covered with colored plastic tins lined the right side. Even more rows of foot-treadle sewing machines filled the left. The lines went back as far as I could see. The building was ten times bigger than anything I had ever ~~seen~~ imagined.

This was definitely no school.

"Come on." The man roughly pushed me forward until we reached a flight of stairs near the wall on the right side. "Go upstairs," he ordered.

I looked back at Samir. Where was my ~~brave~~ arrogant little brother? He had already turned quiet and helpless, following instructions like a domesticated animal.

Of all the unhappy surprises of that day, Samir turning coward may have been the worst. He would not even look at me when the man ordered me to go upstairs. It was as if he knew already what I had not even guessed, that we had been bought to become slaves.

That we were trapped. That there was no way out.

Five

My First Day in the Factory

The sun rose and sent lines of light through the one tiny crack in the wall near my pallet on the floor. I stretched and yawned, wondering what Mother would do to the leftover rice to try to make breakfast interesting. We could fry it with—

Then I remembered. ~~Mother was gone.~~ We were gone. We were hours away from home. The angry man had shoved us both into a small office at the top of the stairs. Then he pushed us on through a door at the end of the office, which led to a tiny room with a tiny window.

"You'll stay here until I decide it's safe for you," he said. He backed out of the room and slammed the door. I heard a key turning the lock from the outside.

"Safe?" I asked. "He wants to make sure we're safe?"

Samir sank to the hard floor. His eyes were already empty. He did not even seem to be holding any anger. I, however, held enough for both of us.

"What he means," Samir said, his voice almost a whine, "is that he will keep us locked up until he knows we won't run away."

Then I understood. It was not us he was trying to keep safe. It was his investment. His property.

At that moment I understood what Samir had already figured out. We were bought to be slaves. The man had lied to our parents, had used their ignorance and poverty, and now we were his to use.

A humming noise filled the air around us. We heard it rising, coming from below. The shrieking alarm sounded again, as it had the day before, and once again I covered my ears.

When the alarm finally stopped its terrible wail, I heard a key being inserted into the lock on the door. The doorknob started turning. I quickly backed away to the farthest corner of the room. Samir remained still, sitting on his mat. I hoped for some measure of strength from his eyes, but he would not look up from the floor.

He was already acting like ~~a good~~ an obedient slave. I wanted to kick him. Where was the boy who laughed at my suffering? Where was the boy who said he could do anything, fight anyone?

The man entered the room, and I had no chance to scream my objections to my brother. When the man kicked Samir and told him to get up, it all made sense. Samir had found a bully bigger than himself.

He was defeated.

Like a trained dog, Samir followed the man from the room. I rushed to exit behind him. Whatever was out there was better than being locked in a tiny room by myself all day long. Or so I thought.

At the top of the stairs, just outside the office, I looked down and felt my mouth drop open. The building was full of children. Children at the sewing machines. Children at the small tables with plastic tins. Even the overseers walking down the rows were children.

"What is this place?" I whispered, wondering whether I really wanted the answer.

The angry man chuckled. It was not a nice sound. "This is my garment factory. Other factory owners hire teenage girls or destitute people from the city. But they have to pay them an adult's pay. I fill my factory with children." He gestured down over the scene as a benevolent king would his kingdom. "Children don't need money. What would they spend it on? Children only need to be cared for. That is what I do. I feed them and provide their clothes. For some, I provide shelter."

Samir's bottom lip was trembling. I scowled. "But some of the children are wearing rags and have no shoes. And where do you house them all? Yesterday they were all running away!"

He narrowed his eyes as he looked down at me. "You are a smart one, aren't you?" He reached out and touched my hair, and I stepped back, feeling afraid sick at the touch. "It's a shame you're not pretty too."

With another gesture out over the hundreds of children, he continued. "I don't have room to house them all, of course, so many of them live on the streets, or they go home to their families—if they have family."

"Why don't they run away?"

He grinned down at me, and I felt myself starting to shake. Something was very bad about this man.

"I was hoping you would ask that," he said, still smiling like a cat that had just caught a fat mouse. "They don't run away because I own them and they know it. If they leave before their debt is paid, I will hunt them down. I know where each child's family is, and I will make the family pay. Or if they live on the streets, alone, that is very dangerous. Many accidents happen every day."

Samir had yet to say one word; he just kept staring at all the kids already working downstairs. I could not stop shaking, but somehow my mouth still worked.

"What debt are you talking about?"

His big belly bounced as he laughed. "Ah, the debt is large. Even you, already, have a considerable debt. The ride here in the auto, your lodging in my building, the money I paid your parents. Then as the days go by, you will owe me for the food you eat, any medicine you need, any clothes I provide."

He rubbed his hand along the banister as a man would a favorite pet. "It takes a very long time to pay off debt." With another chuckle, he started down the stairs, motioning for us to come with him. "Yes, you will belong to me for a very long time." He looked back and his eyes were black. "Maybe forever."

Six

A Garment Factory Slave

The next three years—yes, three whole years—were horrible. I learned to sew in perfect, tiny stitches to avoid being beaten for sloppy work. I learned to work the sewing machine faster and faster to avoid a lash of the whip for being lazy. At first, I would look around, trying to find Samir, only to have the whip slash down on me again.

In time, I turned coward just as Samir had. What good was courage when all it got you was a beating and a night in a locked room? For the first few weeks, I watched and listened and asked questions, trying to think of some way to escape and get back home. Over those weeks, not one child spoke with me. Not one child made a move against the man in the office. Not one child ever left and never came back.

Just as a leaf dropped into a river is carried by the current, so I began to drift away from ~~my goals~~ ~~my courage~~ myself. The days took on a painful routine. I'd hunch down over a piece of clothing, squinting at my work because the boss did not want to waste electricity and thus kept the lights at the lowest setting possible. I sewed on labels covered in words I could not understand. I created pieces of clothing so foreign to me that I could not even guess what they were for.

One day, after I had been in the factory for several weeks, I was assigned a machine next to a girl who actually talked to me. "Where are you from and how did you end up here?" she asked.

I was so surprised to hear another person's voice—I had started talking to myself in my head just to help pass the time—that I just stared at her a full minute.

"Don't look at me," she whispered. "They will notice. Keep your eyes on your work and we can talk if we're quiet."

I quickly set my gaze back on the table, where a very odd garment awaited my attention. It was large, bright green, and stuffed with something that made it puffy all over. After I told my story to the girl and she told me hers—she had been sold by a distant cousin who had offered her a ride to school one day—I asked her, "Do you have any idea what this thing is for?"

She giggled. "It's called a snowsuit. It is for Americans to use when they go skiing."

"What is snow?" I asked. Americans I had heard of. I wondered why we were making their clothes. They lived very, very far away. "What is skiing?"

The girl giggled again. "The snowsuit is to keep you warm in the winter. Winter is the cold season in America. And skiing is sliding on the snow while standing on two long sticks."

I was more confused than before. Sliding while standing on sticks? "Well, I know for certain it will keep someone warm. I am dripping with sweat just working on it."

She sighed. "Yes, these places are not called sweatshops for nothing."

I had never heard of a sweatshop before. I wanted to ask her more, to remind her she had not yet told me what snow was, but the alarm sounded above our heads. I don't know whether I had gotten used to the horrible sound or my hearing had been damaged from the noise, but I no longer bothered to cover my ears.

By the time I looked up, the girl was gone. Every chair in the building was empty. Every chair except mine. Even Samir's was empty. The boss had seen that Samir was already broken, so he let him go outside the building at the end of the day. I was still forced to sleep in the upper room, with the door locked from the outside. Though I envied Samir his freedom, breathing in fresh air and walking around, I knew that being ~~allowed~~ sent from the building was not the luxury I'd imagined. In a rare moment together, Samir had told me he had been forced to find a place on the streets to sleep.

A shiver ran through me. Sleep on the streets? Who knew how many bugs or rats or other terrible things were out there? And how would you keep warm at night? Samir certainly had no snowsuit like the one I was making.

For a fleeting second I considered stealing it and giving it to Samir, but that thought was quickly doused by the reality of what would happen to me if I were caught. Which I surely would be.

I scowled, then sighed. What good was courage if you had no chance to use it?

Seven
Let Out of the Building

At the end of three years, after I turned thirteen, the boss finally ~~kicked me out~~ decided that I could leave the building at the end of the day. He and I both knew I was still not broken, but he needed the upper room for a new set of children he had brought in. Looking at their faces, full of confusion, still carrying a trace of hope, made me sadder than anything ever had. Worse than when one girl's hand got caught in one of the larger machines and part of her finger was chopped off. Worse even than that one day when Samir sat next to me and started crying as he told me how much he missed our parents.

When the alarm sounded that day, I was the first to jump from my chair and run toward the door. I flung it wide open and took in a huge, gulping breath of outside air. It was the first time I had left that closed-in, dark building for three long years. It felt wonderful. I stared up at the sky. I even smiled.

Then a jostling horde of children flooded the air around me. They pushed and shoved, and I was nearly knocked over. A hand grabbed my arm and guided me forward with the crowd. I looked over to see that it was Samir. My brother looked back at me. When had he grown so tall? He would be almost twelve years old by now. He smiled, but it was more like a grimace trying to be a smile.

"Well, now you get to be a street kid like the rest of us," he said. His half smile dropped into a frown. "You need to stick with me, okay? The streets can be dangerous at night."

As we walked together, I wondered what my brother's life had been like the past three years. Those nights I was locked in upstairs, I had missed him. Even his teasing and pinching. Well, not his pinching.

Samir took me to what he called his hotel, a nasty pile of used plastic bags and cast-off clothing under a bridge. "This is where you sleep?" I could feel my face scrunch up.

"Would you rather sleep out there?" He pointed to the sidewalk near the road, where two beggars were fighting over a scrap of food they had found in a trash pile. Several other women beggars held squalling babies. When a vehicle stopped at the red light nearby, the whole group surrounded it, their hands out.

"No," I said quietly. I did not want to beg. Even as low as we'd become as slaves, I was not that low yet.

That night, as Samir snored and I lay awake, unable to sleep with all the noise and lights of the city, I began forming a plan in my mind. We could escape one night, and since they would not know what had happened until the next morning, we would have a good head start. If we could figure out where our home was and where we were now, we could maybe sneak onto a train and get home in time to warn our parents about the boss. Then our whole family could pack up and leave, moving somewhere he would never find us.

I finally slept, and in the morning I forgot to tell Samir my plan. When I remembered, as we walked toward the factory, I decided I would wait. He was whistling a little, and I did not want to make him angry. An escape plan shouldn't make him angry, but who knows how a boy thinks? So I stayed quiet and listened to his happy tune. We would have plenty of time to talk later.

Or so I thought.

eight
The Fire

That day started out tedious and uncomfortable as usual. I sat in my assigned chair, my back already aching after just an hour or so. I was stitching labels onto pieces of clothing my one friend called jeans, yet another item for Americans. Why didn't Americans make their own clothes? Here we all were, making clothes for Americans, but none of us were allowed to make clothes for ourselves. That didn't seem ~~right~~ fair.

I longed to stand up and stretch. I wished for a glass of water. But I asked for neither, knowing such questions would only earn me pain. Literally.

Instead, I hunched back over my work, sewing on small white labels that my friend told me said, "Made in India." I could not read them because they were written in English, the language Americans speak. It somehow made me feel better, knowing the Americans would know the clothes they wore came from here. From me. I wanted to find a pen and write my name on the labels, to find some way to say, "I am here! I am trapped in a box of brick, making your clothes. Don't forget me!"

I was smiling inwardly at the idea when I heard the shout. My head went up and I looked around. Other children were doing the same, all with the same confusion on their faces as I'm sure was on mine. Every day here was exactly the same. No talking. Nothing but work. Definitely no shouting allowed.

Another shout. I could not make out the words. A scream came from far down the row. I saw kids all over that area jumping up from their chairs and running. Running toward me, then past me, toward the door.

What were they doing? "Do you want us all to be beaten to death?" I said to one boy rushing past.

He yelled only one word as he ran by me, but that one word filled me with such terror that I fell from my chair.

"Fire!"

By then children all over the factory were scrambling in a panic toward the door. I felt myself being pushed by a hundred bodies. I could not breathe. "Open the door!" I tried to shout but could not even hear myself over the cries of so many others.

"It's bolted shut!" I heard someone say. As the panic around me began flooding inside me, I looked around. No exits. No windows. No escape route.

What could we do? I looked back and saw the flames rising and moving, like a living monster seeking out its prey. It headed right toward us, eating up the tables and chairs as it came.

Were we all going to die?

nine
Escape

The alarm sounded. Its volume silenced all of us. We looked around; we looked up. Why had the alarm gone off? It was not anywhere near time for the day to be over.

In the silence I could hear the fire cracking pieces of wood and disintegrating them. Sweat beaded up across my forehead. My lungs filled with smoke, and I began coughing.

Suddenly, the boss was in the midst of us. He was shouting at everyone to get out of his way. I looked up the stairs. He must have been in the office. He must have sounded the alarm. And now he needed to go through those double doors to get out, just as we did. If he kept us trapped inside, he would die too.

The double doors opened. We held hands up to shield our eyes from the bright sunlight even as we fled forward, away from the fire.

From the corner of my eye, I noticed the boss screaming as he waved his hands, "Stop! Stay where you are. All of you! Listen to me!"

None of us stopped. None of us listened. We ran, taking our opportunity for freedom.

I had to find Samir. Now was our chance! "Samir!" I called my brother's name over and over again in the crowd. "Samir, where are you?"

We could go find our parents and be a family again. Surely Father would understand what a terrible mistake he had made. Just the thought of being with my mother again brought tears streaming down my soot-covered face.

Like fingers from a hand, the horde of children spread in all directions, and I finally saw Samir ahead of me, looking around. Was he looking for me? There were at least ten people between us. "Samir!"

He rushed to me. "Are you okay?" His voice was gruff, as if he had breathed in some of the smoke.

I tilted my head to the side to say yes, smiling up at him. After several seconds, he smiled back.

We journeyed together, away from the burning building and toward the pile of plastic bags he called home. "Samir, I have a plan about how we can—"

My speech was cut short as we turned the corner and I rammed right into someone big and tall.

"Pardon me," a voice said above me. "You two look like you could use a bath."

I looked up to see a man, probably around the age of my father, smiling down at me. His dark hair was wavy, and his suit was very fine. When he spoke, his voice reminded me somehow of the ripples on the ocean when the wind settled down to a soft, gentle breeze.

He seemed so nice, so different from the boss. I smiled up at him. "We just escaped from a fire in a factory."

"Escaped, huh?" The nice man rubbed his chin. "Did you work at the factory? Are you needing new jobs now?"

I looked over at Samir, who was warily studying the man. "We might be," he said. "Why?"

"I might be able to help you." His smile never wavered, and his voice was smooth. "I am the owner and manager of a rock quarry outside the city. I could use two strong young people."

Samir looked over at me, as if asking my opinion. At first I didn't know what to say. I wanted to get back home as quickly as possible to warn our parents about the boss. Then I realized that we would need money, not only to travel back home but to help our parents move somewhere else. Would it be a good idea to work for a while first? Surely the boss would not go find our family first. He would go to the families living close by before ours.

"Maybe we could work there for a while, just long enough to save up some money for my plan."

"Your plan?" Samir asked.

"Yes, I—"

"Well, splendid," the nice man said, rubbing his hands together. "I have my car right here. Why don't you come with me and I'll show you where you will work?'

I eagerly got into the back seat, excited about my first car ride ever.

And that was how we were trafficked the second time.

ten
Slaves Again

My hope started fading the moment we arrived at the quarry. The nice man handed us over to someone he called the foreman. Then he patted each of us on the head, got back in his fancy car, and rode away.

The foreman was not smiling; his words were not smooth. Soon we joined a host of other children who spent all day pounding rocks into gravel. It was outside work, under the hot sun, with no breaks for lunch or even water. My throat dried out. Every inch of my skin, hair, and clothes became covered with grey dust from the rocks. I had blisters on both hands by the end of the first day.

At night, all of us children slept in one room of a shack at the edge of the quarry. The quarry area was so vast I could not find the place where we came in. I could see no gate, no entrance or exit, and my renewed courage sank as if weighted down with buckets of the gravel I pounded.

It was hopeless.

Day after day that word pounded into my mind, pounded along with the sound of my hammer against rock. It echoed in the sound of a hundred other hammers pounding a hundred other piles of rock. Hopeless. Hopeless.

I did not bother to cry. My body was so dry I could not have produced tears had I tried. We worked from the time the sun rose until after it sank; then we trudged back to the building, looking like a band of ghosts come back from the dead. Only we were not ghosts. We were children, covered in grey dust, walking like old people under the strain of despair.

After a while I stopped keeping track of days and weeks and months. What was the use? There was no way out for any of us. We were trapped on that hill of rock just as much as we had been trapped in that factory. Were the gods punishing me for something I had done in a past life? It was bad enough that I was born a girl. What could I possibly have done to deserve this?

I wondered about my parents. Whether they missed us. Whether they sat near the sea at night and talked about how they regretted ~~selling us~~ sending us away.

Imagining their remorse, I nearly smiled, until I realized with a jolt that I could not picture their faces any longer. It had been over three years. Would I know them if I could make it back home? They certainly would not know me. Three years had changed my girl's body into the body of a woman. Almost. My hair had grown, and I was taller. If I could ever get the dust off me, I think I might even be pretty. I saw my reflection once in a sheet of metal in the factory. The metal distorted my image, but I saw enough to know that I wasn't unattractive. Would my father notice me now that I had grown up? I was thirteen, old enough for him to start arranging a marriage for me. I know he would hate having to pay a dowry, but surely he would be a little proud to see me, wouldn't he? Especially if I were the one who had arranged our escape and brought his son back home?

My thoughts were interrupted when a car drove up to the edge of the quarry. I recognized it, and my teeth bared in anger. The man who had seemed so nice stepped from the vehicle. Another man, whose shirt stretched over his muscled arms, stepped out behind him. They looked all around the quarry. Then the first man said something to the second, and they both laughed.

My stomach crunched up. Something bad was going to happen. I just knew it.

eleven
Sold Again

It happened again. I was sold. The man with the smile, who looked so kindhearted, turned me and several other girls over to this stranger. "Don't worry, they'll all be quite pretty once they get a bath," he said with a laugh.

The new man, the one with the muscles, looked us over as if he was in the market and we were slabs of meat. He turned one girl around, scanned her from head to toe, then shook his head. "No, not this one." She went back toward the pile of rocks.

He looked over another, then another. When he came to me, I don't know what came over me, but the moment his hand reached out to turn me or touch me or poke me, I spit at him. Right in his face. Maybe I hadn't lost my courage after all. Maybe it had just been hiding beneath all this hateful dust.

The first man shouted in anger and was ready to strike me, but the muscled man held up a hand. He grinned. "I'll definitely take her. I like the ones with fire still in them."

Fire. The word reminded me of the day Samir and I escaped the factory. Where was Samir? I looked behind me to the mountain of never-ending rock. He was halfway up the incline. He had stopped his work and stood, watching, a metal bucket in one hand and a hammer in the other.

His eyes were so far away I could not see what was in them. I think it was sadness. Maybe a little worry. Just the thought that he would worry, that someone in this world cared about what happened to me, filled me with some kind of ~~happy good~~ almost hopeful feeling. I tried to communicate with my eyes. Tried to tell him that I was going to escape. That I would come back to find him someday.

Three other girls and I were ushered into the car. I looked out the window to see the muscled man handing a wad of bills to the first man, who was still smiling. How could he smile when he was selling people as if they were animals? How could his heart not be tearing in pieces at the evil he was doing?

Muscle man got into the front passenger seat and ordered the driver to go to a certain address. "Too bad we couldn't get you a bath before we left," the man said. "You're getting dust on the seats."

The girl next to me started crying. Her teardrops hit the dust on her worn dress and made tiny mud puddles. I wanted to comfort her but did not know how. What good thing did I have to say anyway?

"Don't worry," I finally said, very softly so the men in the front seat could not hear. "Maybe we can all escape together."

"Escape?" The girl on the other side of the crying girl leaned over. Her voice was hard and old. "Don't you know where we're headed? Don't you know what's going to happen?"

"No." I shrugged a little, embarrassed by my ignorance.

"Fool," the girl said. She talked even though her teeth were clenched together. "This guy bought only girls, and the only ones he considered were those of us who were pretty." She clenched her hands in her lap. "Labor trafficking is only half of this business. The other side is much worse."

"Worse?" How could anything be worse than slaving away in a factory or in a rock quarry? "What do you mean?"

"What they will sell is not our labor but our bodies," the crying girl whispered. "They're going to force us to become prostitutes."

#
Not Me

I felt dizzy and almost threw up. What were they talking about? I didn't know what a prostitute actually had to do, but I had enough of an idea to know the one girl was right—it was worse than labor trafficking.

And it wasn't going to happen to me. We were now in the city, and I knew it was now or never. The first stoplight that turned red was my chance. I threw open the car door, jumped from the vehicle before it had fully stopped, and ran. Faster than I knew I could, I ran through rows of market stalls, around corners, under hanging clotheslines, all with men running and shouting behind me.

Out of breath, panting, I turned one more corner and found myself at a dead end. I was surrounded on three sides by walls, with the only way out being the way I came in.

No. No! I could not be captured. Not again. Not for their purposes.

I heard voices. Shouts. Someone was asking a street vendor which way I had gone. I did not have much time. I saw a pole running up one of the walls and began climbing. My foot slipped. My hands scraped down the wall and bled. I ignored the pain and tried again but could not get a foothold.

They were coming. "God help me!" I shouted. I do not even know to which of the hundreds of gods I prayed. Whichever one would listen.

A door suddenly opened in the wall right beside me. Someone must have heard my distressed prayer. A woman peeked out, saw me covered in dust, looked down the alley, and heard the shouts. With not one second to spare, she pulled my arm until I was inside, then shut the door.

"Thank you," I said, still panting. I am not sure whether I was thanking the woman or the gods. Maybe both.

"What on earth has happened to you, child?" Her eyes looked from my bare feet to my worn clothes to the dust covering my face and hair. I gasped out my story, my bleeding hands still shaking. The more I said, the farther downward her mouth curved.

"Come with me," she said when I had finished. A loud banging on the door had me immediately right behind her. She led me to a room near the back of the house. "Get cleaned up," she whispered. "I'll deal with those men."

I did not utter one word of protest as she shut the door and closed me in, though for all I knew she could be a trafficker too. Every adult I'd met in this city so far was. But even if she were, I was willing to take the chance. Anything to get away from those men and what they were planning to do with me.

She had said to clean up. I looked around the tiny room. It was completely covered in blue ceramic tile. On the left side was a square tile enclosure that held water in it. A dipper floated on the top. On the right side was a very curious thing. A hole in the floor, but not a hole by accident. It was there on purpose, I could tell that. The hole had a small section of ceramic on each side. Once I saw the small sections were for my feet, I realized this was just a fancy place to squat and relieve myself.

I had never seen one before. We had nothing like this in our one-room bamboo shack. We just had to go outside and find a private place, or use a bucket during the night. I never liked that, because then you had to empty it the next day.

At the garment factory, a set of large buckets had sat in the back corners of the building, but I learned my first week there to drink as little water as possible in the morning so I could make it through the day without visiting them. If the smell wasn't motivation enough, the sting of a whip on the way there or on the way back was. And because the buckets were emptied only at the end of the week, after two or three days the smell actually became the worse of the two.

I marveled at the new contraption, and then my gaze wandered to the square filled with water. Was this what I was meant to use to clean myself? Should I climb inside?

A knock on the door made me jump. I let out a little squeal, then slapped my hand over my mouth. What if it was the men, looking for me?

I kept completely still and silent until the woman's voice assured me that the men were gone. "I work at an orphanage. You have nothing to fear from me. I try to help children." I was safe. Only then did I remove my hand from my mouth and breathe again.

"Excuse me," I said, feeling very foolish. "How—how am I to use . . . how am I to clean myself in here?"

"Oh," the woman said. "You just pick up the dipper, fill it with water, and then pour the water over yourself."

I stared at the dipper floating on the water. One dipper full would not clean all the dirt that caked my hands, much less my body. And I did not want to even think about my hair. It had grown down below my shoulders and was filthy.

Perhaps the lady figured out that I was ignorant because she then added, "Take off your clothes, and then use the soap and however much water you need to get clean."

So that was how it worked. "Thank you!"

I cannot express how good it felt to scrub layer after layer of dirt from my face and body. It had been so long since I had been able to take a bath.

Enjoying the feeling of the cool water running over my skin, I relished every moment of my bath. Except for trying to get the dirt out of my hair. It was a miserable tangle from weeks of not brushing it.

Just as I was finishing, the woman's voice returned on the other side of the door. "I'm putting a clean outfit just outside."

"For me?" I was astonished. Why was this stranger being so nice to me? Was it a trap?

"For you. I used to wear it, but now it is too small."

When her voice faded and I could tell she was gone, I opened the door a crack, snatched up the outfit, and then shut the door again. My eyes greedily looked over the soft blue material of the woman's *shalwar kameez*. It looked new, much nicer than anything I had ever worn in my life. "I will feel like a princess in this," I whispered to myself, putting on the baggy pants and tying the string at the waist. The fresh cotton was a soft caress down my arms as I put on the long top. Last, I wrapped the extra scarf from one shoulder to another, being sure to cover up the new curves developing on my body. I did not want to attract any more attention. Attention was a bad thing in this city.

Timid as a frightened baby kitten, I stepped from the little room and saw the woman waiting in the hall for me. She smiled, then looked behind me to the pile of dusty clothing. "Let's just get rid of those things," she said, briskly passing me and gathering up my old clothes. "That new outfit looks lovely on you."

She went somewhere with the clothes and came back with empty arms. After motioning me to sit, which I did, she also sat and looked me over.

"Now that I have you and those men don't, let's talk about what we're going to do with you."

I hung my head. I knew it. She was going to use me too. Was there anyone good in this whole city? In the world?

thirteen
Running Away

I almost did not listen to the woman's words; I was too full of ~~fear~~ discouragement. But when she started describing the orphanage where she worked, I looked up and started paying attention. Her words spoke of a safe place, a place to learn, even time to play with other children.

It sounded like a dream. "I will take you there right now," the woman said. "It would be good for you to leave this area, considering those men will likely keep looking for you around here."

I gulped. "Yes, that is a good idea. Thank you."

The woman summoned an auto, and we rode for a while. As each mile passed, I debated inside myself. Should I tell her that I cannot stay at an orphanage, that I must go home to find my parents and then have them help me find my brother? Should I ask for her help in finding my family?

No, I would not tell her anything. It was too much of a risk. She seemed kind and had helped me, but I would not give her information that could be used against me in the future. I made my decision just as the auto stopped in front of a gate.

"Let's go inside and get you settled." The woman stepped out and paid the taxi driver. She looked up at a sign above the entrance—Kolkata Christian Orphanage. Love God, Love Others—then turned back to smile at me.

A heavy guilt filled me. I did not want to seem ungrateful. "Thank you for helping me," I said, choking over the words. She was the first person to be nice to me in years. I felt my eyes stinging.

Something in me wanted to beg her to let me stay with her, to pretend she was my mother, to stay safe, to have food to eat, to have an entire room just for getting clean.

But I had to find Samir and my parents. I could not stay in an orphanage or even with her.

"You're very welcome, child . . . but . . . where are you going?"

I had backed away, turned, and started walking away from the gate to the orphanage. I called back over my shoulder, "I'm sorry!"

I ran away. Down streets and through alleys, into the heart of the city of Kolkata, India.

A place, I was to discover, that was full of dangers.

Fourteen
Street Kid

I was alone. Cold. Scared.

I used to imagine how fun it would be to be on my own. No one telling me what to do. The freedom to make friends with a street kid, have an adventure, or wander through the market as long as I wanted.

Back then, my imagination created all sorts of wonderful scenes of how I would spend my time. However, even in my imagination, the freedom I yearned for was only for an hour or two. Then I would return to my home and my life.

I never wanted to be on my own forever. But now, before I had the chance to even talk with a street kid in this city, I became one.

This was nothing like the adventure I had dreamed of. I wandered through the market, but it was no fun without any money to buy anything. I wandered through the busy streets. So much noise. So many people. People ~~walked around me~~ who did not notice me or pushed me out of their way.

Night began to fall, and as the moon rose, so did my fear. Where would I sleep? What would I do?

Finally, I found a bridge and took a place under it. There were others there, beggars and street kids who stared at me, the newcomer. But I had no wish to make friends or share my story. I was tired and hungry and cold. I pulled my knees up to my chest and sat waiting. Waiting . . . though I knew there was no one to wait for.

Looking up at the moon, familiar but cold, I sniffed and felt tears coming to my eyes. No, I would not cry. Samir would get angry, and—

I put my head down on my knees. Samir was not there. My parents were not there. What would it matter if I cried?

So I did. My shoulders shook. I cried out my grief at having my childhood taken away, at being sold like a trinket, at being rejected by my father. Darkness fell. Two crows fought and complained on a pile of trash near my feet. A goat wandered from the street to snatch a ripped newspaper page from the pile. It chewed lazily, not seeming to notice its supper wasn't actually food.

As the lonely minutes became hours, my tears dried and in the place now emptied of tears rose a deep and terrible hatred. I hated them all—the traffickers, the other children who never tried to escape, my brother, the parents who sold me. And the gods. I hated all the gods and goddesses. I did not even know the names of them all, but I hated every one of them with a force so strong it filled my body with heat.

I lay down, full of a new energy. This blanket of hatred would keep me warm at night there under the bridge. Maybe it would help me find food during the day. I suddenly had no desire to find my parents or Samir. Why should I? I was the one lost alone. Someone should come and find me instead.

I was done caring about other people. I was done asking the gods for help.

No one would help me but myself.

Dear Samir,

I've been writing for hours, yesterday and today. It has taken me longer than I thought to tell ~~our story~~ my story. Auntie Asha was right: putting it all down into words does make things clearer. But she also said it would help me see the truth from the lies. So far all I can see are lies. Maybe truth is in there somewhere, but I have not found it yet.

I decided to take a break from the story to tell you about the pizza and this house and the strange ways of the people who live in it. I know I'm using the word "strange" too much, but that seems the best word for my life since we ~~went away~~ were taken away. At this point, I am not sure I know what not-strange would look like.

About the pizza, you would love it. It is like a huge paratha topped with lots of cheese and sauce and little, round pieces of red meat that look very foreign. But there was no rice on it at all! That supper was the first time in my life I ate a meal that did not have rice. I asked Auntie Asha if we could have pizza again. She smiled and said yes. Then she said that ~~if~~ when we found you, we could have pizza and even ice cream to celebrate.

Auntie Asha is very nice, and her husband, Mr. Mark, is different from any man I have ever known. They are married, but they are also best friends. I can tell. When they smile at each other, it is like they forget the rest of the world. I sneaked to spy on them one day and saw them both in the kitchen washing the dishes. Together. Can you imagine? He was actually helping her. Then Mr. Mark put his arms around her and kissed her on the forehead. Then he kissed her on the mouth, right there in the kitchen!

I must have squeaked or squealed a little because they broke apart, but then they both smiled at me, and I could see they were not angry with my spying.

"Come in and help me dry the dishes, please," Auntie Asha said to me. "My husband has to get back to work, and I could use your help."

Timidly, I walked in, making a wide arc around the man with yellow hair. I still don't quite feel comfortable around all that white skin yet. He grinned at me, then at her. He almost kissed her again, but I think he remembered I was there watching, so he winked at her instead before he left.

Oh my. I'm not sure I can handle all the love in this house. I've been here several days now, and I have not heard them yell at each other even once. They disagree sometimes, and Mr. Mark calls Auntie Asha headstrong—what does that mean, I wonder, that her head is strong?—but then he smiles at her like she's a brand-new motor scooter. They talk about things without shouting or throwing things. And they pray all the time to Auntie Asha's God, who they say made everything. Every time we eat, they thank Him for giving them food.

"You are the one who worked to get the food," I said once. "Why thank a god for something you earned?"

I had put my head down, expecting to be rebuked for asking questions, but Auntie Asha seemed happy that I asked instead of angry. "That is an excellent question, Jasmina," she said. I dared to look up at her. "The holy book, the Bible, says that every good gift is from God. Even though we work to earn food or money, in the end, it is God who gives us the strength to work, the ability to make money, and He is the one who makes things grow. So everything we have that is good ultimately comes from Him. That is why we thank Him."

Strange. I am going to try to stop using that word so much. But what other word can describe how things are in this half-Indian, half-American house?

I changed the subject then and asked Auntie if there was any rice at all in America. She laughed and said yes, there was, but not in bags as big as we buy here. She says Americans eat rice sometimes, but other times they eat bread or noodles or hamburgers and something called french fries.

I asked her what a french fries is and she smiled at me. I can't figure out why she keeps doing that. "Would you like to help me cook some tomorrow for supper?"

Right then I got that awful desire to cry again. Ever since I arrived here, I keep finding reasons not to be angry and not to hate. I remind myself that I have to be tough, strong, and fueled by anger, but how can I when I am staying in a place of such peace and happiness?

No, it is more than just happiness. It is a kind of joy that I think they would still have even if the roof caved in or a fire destroyed their home . . . or someone like me, full of hate, came to live with them.

I wish I knew how to talk to Auntie's God. I would ask Him to bless her and Mr. Mark for not selling me or hitting me or making me into their slave.

Whose slave are you now, Samir? I told Auntie Asha about the quarry. She has been asking around to find out how many rock quarries are near the city. She says she will help me find you, but then she adds, "God willing," and that confuses me. How does God have anything to do with it if we do all the work?

Even so, I wish I could ask Him to help us. If Asha's God does run the universe, it sure would help to have power like that. We're going to need a lot just to find you, and even more to get you free.

They just called me to come have a snack, so I will have to stop writing for tonight. I will start again tomorrow.

Oh, Samir, it is so wonderful not being hungry all the time. Yesterday, snack was fresh pineapple and mango juice. Delicious. Whatever it is today, I know it will be good.

If you were here, I would share some with you. Maybe.

Your sister,
Jasmina

Fifteen
Hungry

I decided I must not be a very good street kid. Everything hurt. Sleeping on the street, or rather under a bridge, was not nearly as fun as I'd imagined it would be. Concrete is just hard, not fun. And the street is noisy all night. Do the people in the city not sleep at all? What woke me up this time?

A finger jammed into my ribs again.

"Ouch!" I sat up, rubbing my side.

"That's my spot," a dirty, barefoot boy said. He leaned over me, and his face was not friendly at all. "Move on."

I wanted to tell him he couldn't command me. He wasn't my father.

Not that my father would care. He didn't even know that I was here, lost and alone and so very hungry.

"I said move on."

The boy's face came down near mine. The ~~pain~~ fear in my eyes did not affect him. His mouth became an angry thin line.

I scurried backward, away from the boy. He sent me one last vicious look before lying down right where I had been sleeping. What was so special about that spot of sidewalk?

I heard myself whimpering so I bit my lip, determined not to cry again.

Like a bug trying to protect itself, I curled up into a ball. Soon I fell back asleep, though I knew it would not be for long. The morning would come. And with it, all the reasons I wanted to cry.

But I was determined not to. Never again. If I was going to make it on the streets, I would have to become tougher, harder, able to feed off anger as others fed off food. I would rely on myself only. Never trust anyone again. Never give in to the weakness of hope.

That night I gave up the last piece of my childhood. I threw away the final unbroken portion of my heart.

I slept, knowing that the following day I would become a thief, a pickpocket, a criminal. And I did not care . . . almost.

Over the next two weeks I learned the game of surviving on the streets of Kolkata. I stole food when I was hungry. I stole money from rich tourists' pockets when they weren't looking. My beautiful blue outfit became dirty. My hair matted into tangles again. I learned to scurry away like a cockroach into the darkness when men's eyes would look over my body.

I became hard. As hard as the concrete I slept on every night. Hatred and anger kept me going, made me shove smaller street kids aside without compassion so I could get to thrown-away food first. I would steal from a market stall and run, leaving other street kids to take the blame. I became very good at being bad.

Sometimes, in the night, I would feel remorse for what my life had become. Most of the time, though, I told myself it was my father's fault for selling me. It was my mother's fault for letting him. It was the gods' fault for not giving me any other choices. It was even Samir's fault for not being smart enough to think of an escape for us.

The world became a dark and ugly place, and I found my spot in it.

Until the day I saw the baby, and everything changed.

sixteen
An Unusual Group of Women

I had just stolen a ripe mango from a market stall. Around the corner I ran, laughing at how easy it was to outwit adults. They chased me, but they were so busy flailing their arms and yelling that they did not think ~~hard enough long enough~~ smart enough to ever find me.

When the shouting faded to the left, letting me know they had gone the wrong way, I slid my back down against a wall and prepared to enjoy my snack.

That was when I saw the group of women. What were they doing in this part of the city? They were not dressed like the women of the red-light district, which I just realized I had chosen as my sanctuary again. It was a good place to hide from the good people. Terrible place to try to hide from the bad ones, though. Some of the people who owned the women and children trapped inside the buildings were frightening just to look at. Such hatred. Such purpose.

Would I end up looking like that before too long? Would I eventually not care about anyone and put others through horrible suffering so I could live comfortably?

Suddenly my stolen mango did not taste so good. It soured in my mouth as I chewed. I spit the bite out and tossed the rest to my side, knowing another street kid would find it later and enjoy every last bite.

My eyes went back to the small group of women. Their heads were covered, which in the district area meant they were not the women forced to sell themselves. So then what were they doing crossing the bridge into the worst section of buildings in the whole district? Aside from the trafficked women, who were rarely let out of their rooms, only those who paid were allowed to cross the bridge into the section of brothel buildings. If they weren't trapped slaves, why were they in the red-light district at all? And why were they smiling? There was nothing to smile about in this part of the city.

I stood and crept toward the bridge. I stopped far enough back so the guard at the bridge could not see me but I could still see the group of women. There were six of them, each carrying a book. They walked down the outside edge of one of the buildings. I walked on my sidewalk parallel to them, the open sewer ditch spanning several feet wide between us. The smell of rotting sewage was terrible, but I had been in the city long enough to barely notice it. My attention was focused on the women. What were they doing? What did they want?

Then they did a very surprising thing. They all stopped outside one door, number 114. They stood in a circle, took each others' hands, and then lowered their heads and closed their eyes.

It looked like . . . surely not . . . they couldn't be praying, could they?

seventeen
The Baby

Who were they praying to? What were they praying for?

I could not squelch my curiosity. I had to know what was going on. Stepping quietly and slowly, I moved toward the sewer ditch. Its span was so wide that even if I jumped I would never make it across. The traffickers likely did that on purpose to keep people from escaping.

Unable to get any closer, I stood at the edge of the sewer and watched. One woman said, "In Jesus' name, amen," and then they all lifted their heads and opened their eyes.

I almost called out, "Who is Jesus? What does *amen* mean?" But the women had all turned their backs to me. One knocked on door 114. It opened, and all the women went inside.

What were they doing there?

I wanted to know, so I sat down to wait. It wasn't as if I had anything better to do. For an hour I sat pondering what possible explanation there could be for a group of clean, well-dressed, happy women to be coming on purpose to a place of such filth and sorrow and hopelessness.

When the door opened I jumped to my feet, almost slipping and falling into the ditch. I took two steps back, holding my nose. Just the thought made me gag.

"We have one more stop," one of the women said. At that the women seemed to immediately become sad. I heard "I wish we could just snatch her and run" and then "Every time I see her my heart breaks." All the women nodded and more than one brushed away a tear.

I stared and marveled. What could be so bad that women who smile in a brothel would cry over it?

The group walked down the street beside the building, not noticing that I continued walking alongside them. I was still across the ditch, and none of them seemed to be paying attention to anything around them. At the corner of the building, they stopped and once again joined hands, formed a circle, and bowed their heads.

Just as the curious questions nearly burst from my mouth, the women stopped what they were doing and turned around the corner of the building. I could no longer see them. I ran to where the sewer ended at a concrete wall jammed with trash and filth. The wall stood grey and unfeeling between me and the buildings. I ran alongside it until my path was blocked by a tiny roadside store and a few parked rickshaws. Circling around them took me onto the road, where I had to dodge autos and duck when one irritated rickshaw *wallah* took a swipe at me. Once safely past, I saw where the concrete wall ended, parallel with the end of buildings.

Another bridge with another guard marked the end of the collection of brothels. Behind the guard was a small, open concrete courtyard of sorts, connecting the three larger buildings.

The women were clustered around something on the ground. When the group shifted to speak with a woman nearby, I saw what they were looking at. I covered my mouth with my hand. Despite all I had seen in the factory, in the quarry, or on the streets, my mind wanted to say that what I saw could not be real. Not even in this part of the city.

The women had gathered around a baby, maybe one year old, sitting on the ground. The baby did not move. Even from a distance I could see dark bruises along her arms. The thing that made me want to weep, though, was the red rope tied around one of her tiny ankles. It ran only a few feet to where it was knotted around a pole.

She was tied like a dog on a leash.

eighteen
Following Them

I was still staring at the baby when the group of women crossed the bridge and came close enough again that I could hear their conversation.

"It's horrible," one said, uncovering her head and fanning herself. "She won't even consider letting her go."

I wanted to ask who. The baby?

"Asha is in town today, at the compound. Let's go meet with her, pray, and brainstorm about possible strategies."

I did not know at the time who Asha was, or that meeting her would change my life. Their words intrigued me. Were they going to try to help that little child?

Several minutes passed before I realized I was following them again. I continued several meters behind until they arrived at a large metal gate connected to a thick concrete wall. One woman opened the gate just enough to lean her head in. She looked quite comical, her head inside, but her arms gesturing outside. She must be talking with whoever guarded the place, I thought. The wall must enclose houses or other buildings, though I wasn't really curious about the setting. I was trying to figure out how to get inside so I could eavesdrop. The wall was twice my height, so climbing it was not an option. Sneaking in with the women might work, but then what would I do when they discovered my presence inside the walls?

I bit my lip and concentrated, but then the solution actually walked right outside the gate. I watched from a distance as the gate creaked open and a young woman stepped out. She was Indian like the rest of them, with straight black hair and chocolate-colored skin, but her dark eyes shone and her smile made her face nearly as bright as her yellow *shalwar kameez.* She saw the group of women. Her mouth opened with some kind of glad sound, and she hugged several of them. That was unusual. To hug is not very Indian.

I left my hiding place behind a nearby tree and inched closer, close enough to hear her say, "Yes, we should definitely talk through some ideas. I was just walking to the store, and then I planned to get some lunch at that little restaurant nearby. Why don't we all walk together and talk as we walk?"

The women nodded, and they started walking away from the gate like a small herd of sheep, bumping into each other as they all tried to walk side by side on the narrow sidewalk.

Asha—at least I assumed the new lady was the person they had planned to meet—started laughing. "This isn't going to work, is it?" She looked around at her friends. I tried to duck out of sight before her gaze came my way, but I think she saw me. Her voice lowered, but I could still hear the words. "Let's wait and talk at the restaurant."

If she thought that was going to keep me from listening to their plan, she didn't know much about street kids.

The Plan

The restaurant was small, but a collection of fake bushes used for cheap decoration offered a hiding place close enough that I could hear the women's conversation. I scrunched low, hoping I hadn't been spotted. It was uncomfortable, but that did not matter. I was used to being uncomfortable.

"Tell me everything you know so far," the woman called Asha said to the others. They all sat in plastic chairs around a small table, and she ordered chai tea and samosas for everyone. She must be rich. Maybe that was why they wanted to talk with her; maybe she could buy the baby.

"She just turned one year old," one of the women said as she blew into her hot cup of tea. "When she started crawling, the madam did not want her to get away, so she tied her to the pole." The woman sniffed, as I do when I'm trying not to cry.

"Why is she there in the first place?"

"Her mother is only seventeen years old. She was trafficked in from Nepal. She can't speak Bangla and is terrified of the madam."

"Have you talked with the madam?" The Asha woman took a sip of tea. Her eyes had gone from curious to worried. A few weeks before, I would have been surprised to learn that the person who owned that section of the district was a woman. But I had learned that both men and women traffic others. No one could be trusted.

"We tried," another woman answered. When the server brought the snacks, everyone sat silently until the young man was gone. "She won't let the baby go free."

"She wouldn't even let us touch her or hold her," another added, her voice choked with tears. "She says she wants the baby to grow up not knowing what love feels like. She'll be a better worker for her when she gets older if she's never known love."

The woman named Asha put her head down in her hands. I thought she was crying and peeked to see that she was, but she was also praying. The others soon joined her, each speaking very softly, I guess asking their god to help the baby.

I thought of that horrible madam. How much evil would a girl have to suffer to grow into a woman who would do such a thing to an innocent, helpless child? Something inside me started shaking. Was that where my hate would lead me?

"We can't buy her," one of the women said once they finished praying. "That would make us traffickers."

"And we can't grab her and run off with her," added another. "That could ruin all the rescue work we've been doing in that area."

Rescue work? I leaned a little closer to hear better. A plastic leaf from the bush tickled my nose, and I had to hold my breath to keep from sneezing.

"How long have you been going there?" Asha asked.

"Four weeks, twice a week." The first woman, the one who sniffed, answered this time. "We have to pay for our time, but with the time we pay for, the women don't have to . . . um . . . work, and instead they get to hear about how much God loves them and wants them to be part of His family."

God loves them? I almost forgot I was hiding and nearly walked up to their table to ask questions. Did all these women worship the same god? How did they know which one to pray to? And wouldn't the other gods and goddesses get jealous and maybe thwart their plan just out of spite?

Who ever heard of a god loving people anyway? Especially those people.

"So far nine women have already believed in Jesus."

I watched joy spread the lady Asha's face into a wide smile. Whoever this Jesus was, she was happy that they believed in Him. "Praise God," she said. "They may not be free from the brothel, but their hearts and souls are free now, and God willing, one day they will also be free from that place forever."

I had leaned forward a little more, pushing that one leaf aside. When she talked about getting the women free from the district, I gasped before I could stop myself. I saw Asha look around, and I sank lower behind the bushes.

So these women were paying for their time in the district and trying to convince people to try to escape? It was admirable, but foolish. Everyone in the city, even someone as new as I was, knew that once you got trafficked into that district, you never got back out.

twenty
Discovered

The women drank their tea and talked about how they could try to get freedom for the baby who did not even have a name. They just called her Baby. None of their ideas would work. I knew that, and I could tell they knew it too.

After talking long enough to make my legs ache from squatting, Asha finally stood. "None of us can think of any way to help this precious little girl. It seems impossible, but God can do the impossible. Let's all be praying—which is the best thing we can do anyway—that God will deliver this child from evil and give her a life of freedom and hope."

The women rose, nodding in agreement, and then said goodbye to one another and filed out of the restaurant. Asha remained behind. She sat at the table closest to my row of bushes. I scooted over so I could see only her feet, but it must not have been soon enough.

"You can come out now," she said.

I froze. Did she mean me?

"I'm not sure why you were listening to us, but I'd like to talk with you." I thought I heard a smile in her voice. "And you surely can't be comfortable back behind those bushes."

It was me. She had found me out. What was I to do?

Very slowly I peeked from my hiding place. Yes, she was smiling.

I stepped out, but then backed up quickly when the waiter came rushing at me. "What are you doing here? Get out! No street kids or beggars allowed here!"

His arm swung up to hit me, and I flinched, but the blow never came. I opened the eyes I had squeezed shut and saw the woman I had spied on standing between me and the angry man. "It's all right," she was saying. "She's here with me."

Still glaring at me, the man lowered his hand. "Don't let her steal anything," he said before turning away. I guess he felt he needed to have the last word.

By then I was back behind the bushes again, but she came around and stood facing me. Her hand stretched out. "Come. Why don't we take a little walk so we can talk without"—she smiled—"interruptions."

I nodded and once again left my hiding place. As we walked through the little restaurant, I kept my head down so I would not see the people staring and whispering. Once outside, I knew the moment had come when I should run, as I always had. She would not try to catch me, and even if she did, I knew these streets better than anyone, except maybe other more seasoned street kids.

Go. I should go. I should run and not look back. She seemed nice, but I had learned not to trust anyone.

"I saw you watching us back at the compound," she said. Her words surprised me so much I actually stopped thinking of running and waited to hear what she would say next. "And I knew you followed us here." She smiled. "However, I didn't see you find that spot behind the bushes and didn't know you were there for quite a while. Very impressive."

"You knew I was spying on you?"

"Yes."

"How did you notice me? And why aren't you angry?"

Understanding filled her eyes. "I've learned to notice things that most people aren't aware of. And I am not angry because it is obvious you followed us for a reason. I am waiting to find out what that reason is."

While she talked, we had started walking together. I had no idea where we were headed, but I could not get myself to run and leave behind so many unanswered questions. Questions about her and about these women who cried for a baby they were not responsible for. Even still, I stayed wary, glancing around as we walked to make sure we were not headed toward a police station or other places dangerous to street kids.

"You needn't fear," she said when she saw my face. "I am going back to the compound; it is a place where missionaries live. I am visiting my grandmother-in-law and doing some work. No one there has any desire to harm you." She continued before I had a chance to speak. "But before we go inside, I would like to know who you are and why you followed us today. You obviously heard us talking about our work in the brothel and about the baby we want to rescue. What do you plan to do with that information?"

I looked over and saw the same questions in her eyes that I knew were in mine. She was trying to decide whether she could trust me.

A peculiar feeling rose up into my throat, and suddenly I was talking and talking, telling her everything from the first day until now. I will never know why I didn't just run. Why I chose to trust her.

When I had finished, I asked, "Why do you care about the baby? There are hundreds of women and children in that district. Why work so hard to rescue one or two when there will soon be others to replace them?"

My words actually brought tears to her eyes. "You have asked one of the biggest questions of life itself: why bother doing a little good if it doesn't fix everything?" We had arrived at the compound gate, and she stopped just outside of it. "There is no easy answer for your questions, but I think if you come inside, you might discover what you are looking for."

What was I looking for? I just wanted answers to my questions. I felt only idle curiosity. Didn't I?

twenty-one
Something Good

"You picked a wonderful day to come," Asha said as she opened the gate and greeting the guard with a smile. "Today women from our safe houses have gathered together here to celebrate God's goodness and update each other on what is happening in each place."

"Safe houses?" I asked.

"Yes." We were inside before I had made an actual decision on whether I wanted to risk being closed in. Asha was looking at me as if she knew everything about me, which I guess she did since I'd just spilled out my whole story. "You were trafficked and sold," she continued, "and you know what it is like to be treated without worth or love. Today the compound is filled with women and girls just like you. Women who were once trapped, as you were, but who now are free."

We walked toward a large building. I could hear laughter and singing coming from inside.

"You see," Asha said with a smile, "my job, ever since I moved to India, is to rescue girls just like you, and not just rescue them *from* something bad but rescue them *to* something good."

She gestured up the steps to the building. "Will you come with me to meet the others?"

Silently I nodded, and we walked up the stairs toward the door. I did not have much desire to meet other women who had suffered as I had. No, it was not the people that kept me moving forward. It was something she had said that wrapped around my hard heart so tightly I think it cracked wide open.

She rescued girls like me. There were people in the world who wanted to do good instead of evil. There were people who cared about something more than money and power. Who would not use others for their own gain.

Impossible. My mind said not to believe a word. To harden up again and hold tight to hate. But my heart—oh, my heart wanted to think there was hope.

And the thing that gave me the courage to enter that building and face all those strangers, the thing that kept me awake later that night, was one sentence she'd said about not just rescuing victims from something bad but to something good.

What was the something good? And was there any possibility it could be available to me?

twenty-two
A Boy

"*Didi!*" I heard the affectionate term for "older sister" before we had even stepped inside. Asha swung the door open wide, and I saw a boy about my age or maybe a little older, fourteen or fifteen if I had to guess, coming our way. Rumpled hair fell across his forehead, and his face seemed one huge smile. When his shoulder dipped as he took his next step, I noticed he was using a crutch. Looking lower still, I saw why. His left foot was missing. Or rather, it looked like it had never been there.

I had seen kids like him on the streets before, kids who had been born with some kind of defect or harmed purposefully by others because beggars with deformities gained more compassion and therefore more money. This boy's left leg ended with what looked like a small portion of a foot that had never fully developed. Not likely the work of a boss. Just bad luck.

"It's not contagious, you know."

My head shot up quickly, embarrassment turning my cheeks red as fire, to see him grinning at me. A girl just behind him, however, was not. Her chin was up, and her eyes flashed my way. Was she angry that I had stared at his foot? Or was she . . . jealous?

I had no time to mull over this interesting idea because Asha was introducing us. "Milo," as she looked toward the boy, her love for him was as clear as clean water, "I'd like you to meet my new friend Jasmina. She sort of discovered me." She grinned. "You two have a lot in common."

"Ah, another street kid, *Didi?*" His face was open, with nothing to hide. He was no street kid. We street kids all have plenty to hide in every area of our lives, and especially on our faces.

"Did you meet her in front of the ice-cream shop?"

He and Asha both laughed, but I could tell the other girl was as far on the outskirts of the joke as I was.

"And this is Dapika," Asha continued, gesturing toward the girl who still stared at me with suspicion. Not that I blamed her. My face likely held the same wariness.

My gut told me Dapika knew about life on the streets, but this Milo surely did not. He was happy and carefree, joking and smiling, while Dapika and I held ourselves back away from it all, cautious, waiting for something bad to happen.

"Oh, Asha, you're here. I'm so glad!" A woman came rushing by me so quickly I had to catch my balance as I stepped out of her way. She grasped Asha's arm and spoke breathlessly, as if she had been running. "We just got a text. The girl in district three, the one we've been praying for, is on the run."

The air in the large room instantly changed. Women in every direction immediately set down their plates or cups and headed right toward us.

I took another step back, all senses on alert. What was happening?

My wide eyes, certainly full of only half-buried fear, scanned the room and landed on Milo. He caught my eye and grinned as he leaned toward me. "Looks like you're just in time for an adventure!"

"I—I am?" I stuttered. He nodded. Then he winked!

"Have fun," he said.

What?

twenty-three
Swept Up

"She says if we don't get her in fifteen minutes, they'll catch her for sure!"

My mind went back to the garment factory. The hurry and tense excitement around me was like the flow toward freedom every day when the alarm finally sounded. Women were slipping bare feet into shoes they had respectfully left at the door. They all jostled against each other, and I wondered whether any of them were finding their own shoes in the pile or just putting on whichever ones were nearest.

None of these women were acting like victims. They were acting like . . . like . . . I could not think of a word, only a picture. Once on the streets, hungry and alone, I saw a child pull away from his mother and wander toward the busy road. Cars and large yellow taxis and autos and rickshaws all presented a very dangerous threat, but the toddler did not see any of them. He was looking at a cast-off bottle several feet into the road, and he was heading straight toward it.

My heart tightened up, my mind preparing to watch a disaster. But suddenly the mother turned and saw her child, and she became a lioness. Lunging forward, she reached him just in time. I expelled a breath that was both relief and longing. If only someone cared for me like that.

A voice startled me out of my memory. "Oh, you're the girl who was following us today, aren't you?" One of the women from the group had stopped on her way out the door and was staring at me. "I saw you hide behind those bushes at the restaurant." I gasped, but she smiled. She was very beautiful. "I'm Amrita. I was trafficked and forced to work in the red-light district, you know."

I didn't know, but the woman kept talking. "I escaped, and they gave me a safe place to stay. I didn't like them at first." She lowered her voice to a whisper. "Some of them seemed to think being free meant being frumpy, and I am not a woman who likes frumpy. Are you coming with us?"

She half-dragged me out the door, and before I had a chance to even ask, "Coming where?" she started talking again. "Most of the time we're either waiting for word—I work in a beauty salon near the district and keep an ear out for any girls ready to escape—or trying to deal with all the hardships a girl encounters once she's out. You know, like getting off the drugs they force you on or not being able to trust anyone, thinking everyone has ulterior motives or wants something from you."

I gulped. I found myself piling into a taxi with several other women. The one who seemed the eldest gave quick directions to the driver. As we sped away, I noticed other women finding other taxis, autos, or even rickshaws.

"But this is the best part"—the woman named Amrita gestured forward, making the bangles on her arm jingle—"when we get to actually rescue someone just at the last moment."

The woman to my right sighed. "I wish we had more than the last moment sometimes. I'm getting too old for this."

"Oh, Rahab," said yet another woman with a laugh. "You're just worn out from chasing that little Ruth around the Scarlet Cord all day."

Ruth? The Scarlet Cord? How had I ended up in a car with a bunch of women talking nonsense? I was smarter than this. They had all befuddled me with their ~~smiles~~ happiness. Where were the victims Asha had talked about?

And where were we going? Was this all some kind of elaborate ploy to drag me into something terrible?

twenty-four
Singing

"Okay, we're on the right road. Everybody out." Amrita was shoving me out of the taxi with such excitement I could not help but move quickly in response. I looked down the street to see another car door open and several women emerge. They started off toward the right and we headed left. I kept chastising myself the entire time for not just running off and leaving all of them to whatever outlandish adventure they were on.

"Keep an eye out for a girl in red," someone said from behind me. I started looking around. There were people everywhere. How were we supposed to find this girl?

"This should be close. Start singing."

Singing? Was she kidding? I stopped looking for a girl in red and gaped at the women around me, who all suddenly burst into song as if this were some Bollywood musical and we were the main characters. They looked like a bunch of crazy females, singing about being lost but now they were found and blind but now they could see.

I heard the same notes coming from a distance. The other groups of women must be singing the same song. Was this some kind of code?

A hand gripped my arm, hard, and I winced. A shot of fear ran through my body, and I looked over to see Amrita's eyes change from excited to intense. I tried to yank free, but she spoke through tight lips. "Look forward. See the feet under that hanging outfit for sale? At the store on your right?"

I obeyed out of instinct. Sure enough, someone was hiding not half a body length away, and whoever it was had on a red outfit, that much I could tell. My heart started pumping faster, then even faster when I saw several men running in our direction from a nearby road. I knew that sight—it was common enough when someone tried to run away.

I had never seen anyone succeed. They were always caught.

What would these strange singing women do now?

twenty-five
Grab and Go

"Don't look at the men," Amrita whispered to me. "Act like you're out for a fun day of shopping with friends." I looked up at her, my eyebrows arching up almost to my hairline. I was so confused and scared. She hissed out words. "If you keep looking like that, they'll know something is up."

I saw one of the men looking my way and quickly lowered my gaze to my hands, letting Amrita lead me with that iron grip on my arm. We clustered into a circle around the little stall right in front of where the girl hid.

"Oh, I just love this necklace, don't you?"

"No, the beads are uneven, and I don't like the color. This one is better."

The women had stopped singing and were now chattering around me as if none of them were aware of the very near danger. All except Amrita. She inched toward the outfit that hid the girl. I felt the women gather in tighter. A feeling of claustrophobia wrapped around me.

"Are you ready?" Amrita said. I shook my head, then realized she was not talking to me. A fearful, young face peered from behind the hanging outfit only long enough for Amrita and me to see her quick nod, and then she faded back behind the clothing again.

Amrita nodded toward the woman named Rahab, and Rahab immediately motioned for a taxi. "I'm done for the day," Rahab said, much louder than necessary for us to hear her. I tilted my head to look down the road and saw another group of women, also huddled in a circle, turn at her words and head toward another taxi.

When our vehicle pulled up nearby, the women formed a human shield from the hanging outfit to the taxi, blocking any view the searching men might have of me, Amrita, and the young girl as we three dashed from the sidewalk into the back seat of the taxi.

Behind us, several other women toppled in until the seat was more than full. The door shut, and the taxi jerked forward.

"Stay down," Amrita whispered to the girl. I couldn't help crouching down along with her. I felt the girl beside me shaking.

"It's okay," I said, though I don't know why I did. How did I know whether it was okay?

twenty-six
My First Cookie

"Well, what did you think of your first rescue?"

I turned around. How had Milo managed to approach me without my hearing his crutch? Maybe this boy did know something about being a street kid after all.

"My first rescue?" I glanced around, more than a little dazed. "I don't have any idea what is going on here."

Milo grinned at me, and I had a hard time not smiling back. He was so different from what I was used to. When Dapika approached behind him, her eyes and her stance warning me that I was on her territory, I felt much more comfortable. My eyes narrowed to slits. My jaw hardened.

He must have noticed since he turned around and spoke to the girl. "You're not on the street anymore," he said with a soft kind of patience that for some reason made my throat tighten. "You don't have to fight for your place." He nudged her a little with his crutch. "Or your friends."

She looked at him, and then I saw it. She really cared about him. The boy with one foot. The boy with a smile big enough for everyone. She cared, and she did not want to share him.

What would it be like to have a friend like that?

"Come and sit, new girl," Milo said, his tone back to casual and lighthearted. He led the way to the far corner of the room, away from the women huddled like mother hens around the rescued girl—who looked very young and vulnerable. She must have just recently been trafficked and not had time to develop a calloused heart.

We passed a table filled with snacks and drinks and some odd food I'd never seen before. "Do you want something to eat?" he offered.

I shook my head no. Not because I didn't really want anything to eat. Hunger gnawed at me. But I knew better than to do anything that left me indebted to anyone. The price was too high to pay later. Besides, sometimes traffickers drugged a snack or drink to trap new victims.

"It's okay," he said, as if he read my mind. "You're free here, and the food is free too." He laughed at his joke, then sobered at the look on my face. "Really, eat all you want. It's safe, and the people here give it gladly, with no payback expected."

I did not want to show how famished I was, so I slowly put one, then two, then three things onto a plate. The first two things, a *samosa* and a *paratha*, I recognized, but the third was a mystery.

"It's called a cookie." Milo had read my mind again. Or maybe he'd just seen me staring at this unusual round thing with brown spots. "Try it."

He grinned while I took the tiniest bite possible. It was not spicy, as I'd expected, but sweet and soft. "It's American."

American? I swallowed my curiosity about the cookie along with my bite and instead asked the bigger questions on my mind. "What is this place? What is a safe house? What is the Scarlet Cord? And where did all these women come from?"

He laughed. "I hope you're planning to stay awhile because that's a lot of questions."

Dapika, who had been scowling beside him, interjected with a frown, "A safe house is where rescued women go to recover and sometimes live if their families do not want them back. And the women here used to all look as dirty and skinny as you do."

I stiffened when her eyes narrowed and her voice dropped. "Were you in the brothels? How did you get out?"

Milo tapped Dapika's leg slightly with his crutch, a creative way of getting her attention since of course he was not allowed to actually touch her. She looked crossly at him for two seconds, but his tender look, the kind of look I had always wanted to get from my brother, seemed to melt something hard inside her. She slumped down a little in her chair. "Sorry," she mumbled.

I wanted to suggest she shove a very large cookie in her mouth to keep it busy, but I stuck the rest of mine in my own mouth instead to keep down the words I wanted to say. For some incomprehensible reason, Milo did not like fighting and bickering. And for some even more incomprehensible reason, I did not want to make him unhappy. I guess it had been so long since I had seen anyone genuinely happy that I didn't want to be the one to mess it up.

"I escaped all by myself," I said proudly. "And I was not in a brothel."

"Then how did you end up here?" Milo's eyes were curious, and even Dapika lifted her head again to hear my answer.

"I saw some of these ladies all go into the district across the bridge. They all prayed, which was . . . strange."

Milo smiled.

I continued. "Then they all went around a corner, and there was a little baby tied to a pole."

"The baby with no name." Dapika's eyes took on a haunted look. "She'll grow up in that place. She'll watch her mother do drugs and fade away. She'll have no hope of any kind of future outside that piece of hell."

A shiver ran down my spine. Was that what had happened to Dapika?

twenty-seven
The Red Rope

"Oh, Jasmina! I am so sorry!"

I jolted upright in my seat, for a moment expecting a lash on my back for allowing my thoughts to drift.

"Things got so crazy with that girl escaping, and I just let you fall through the cracks, didn't I?"

"Um . . ." I stared up at the woman named Asha, who I just noticed had an unusual accent, and Milo chuckled beside me.

"It means she forgot about you for a little while. It's an American saying."

"Oh." Still dumbfounded into silence, I sat trying to decide whether to ask Asha about the American words and cookies or to ask Dapika what she knew about growing up in a terrible place like a brothel. Did she have a mother or grandmother still trapped there?

Instead, for some reason I blurted out, "The red rope— that's what a scarlet cord is, right? A red rope? Is the Scarlet Cord the place where the baby is tied to the pole?"

The entire room quieted at my words. Every woman turned to stare at me. I sank into my chair, the too-sweet cookie jostling around in my stomach.

A woman rose with a quiet dignity. I remembered her from earlier. She was called Rahab, the one they said chased a little Ruth around the Scarlet Cord all day. Everyone watched in silence, a very unnerving silence, as she walked toward me and, of all things, held out her hand.

"Come," she said softly. "I would speak with you, Jasmina."

Oddly, I felt myself looking to Dapika for reassurance that this woman would do me no harm. Dapika gave a slight nod, so I rose and followed her from the room, outside, toward a small circle of shade made by an obliging tree. We sat, and Rahab began a story that I realized was in layers—a story of her own life and the life of another woman with her same name who had lived many, many years ago. As she wove the story of her own life into this story of a Rahab in a book she called the Bible, she mentioned another red rope. I had a hard time keeping the red rope in the story separate from the red rope she called the Scarlet Cord and the red rope binding a child to a lifetime of slavery.

"Wait. There are too many red ropes," I finally said. "Which is which?"

The woman smiled, and her face was so gentle it was hard for me to believe that she had once been trafficked, a victim, a woman forced to sell herself to survive.

"I'm sorry, child. I get so excited telling about God's grace sometimes that I forget to explain important details."

Again, someone was talking about a god but talking about him as if he were a good and caring one. Something about this place and these people was so unsettling, but so . . . good.

"The red rope in the Bible story of Rahab was very important," she said, using the edge of her sari to fan her face in the sweltering heat. "Rahab the prostitute had believed in God, and God promised to rescue her from the terrible place where she lived. She hung a red rope, a scarlet cord, from her window as a symbol of her faith, and it was to be the sign that not only preserved her life but told the heroes where to find her so she could be saved."

Rahab smiled. "The Scarlet Cord that you have heard the women speak of is the safe house where I live and serve. I named it after Rahab's red rope because I and the other women who live there have been rescued and brought into God's family, restored not only to freedom but to hope. Our lives are like that red rope hung in the window, to let everyone know that God can and does deliver."

"So the red rope tied to the baby isn't really part of this?" I surmised, scooting over to remain under the shade as it shifted with the sun's rays.

"Not exactly." I saw her wipe a tear from her eye. "That precious baby is trapped, and right now we have no way of getting her free." Her eyes began to gleam. "But I believe that red rope is a symbol, just as Rahab's was. That red rope will one day be a sign of freedom rather than slavery. Instead of tying her down, someday it will hang limp and useless, a testament that God delivers."

I looked at this woman who cared so much about a baby not her own. "Your god, he cares about people? Even in places like that?"

Her smile shone as bright as the sunlight around me. "Oh yes, my God cares, and it makes no difference where they come from or what they have done." She sucked in a breath and looked into the distance. "Or what has been done to them. He redeems and restores. He came to set the captives free."

He came? This god, however appealing, had many mysteries.

I opened my mouth to ask another question, but Rahab's direct gaze pierced me into silence.

"Jasmina, you have discovered our secret. We are usually much more careful, but our love for that precious baby made us heedless. Now you know what we do." She looked around. "You also know one of the places we meet, and as of this afternoon, you even know one of our methods—our most creative one." She turned and a seriousness swept over her face. "You now have power over us. Power to harm us and what we seek to do in this city."

She bit her lip, and I was surprised at how young it made her appear. When she looked back at me, I waited, knowing whatever she would say was significant.

"This is not official, as we must discuss it as a group and come to a conclusion, but I would like you to consider staying with us, even if only for a little while. I can see your heart has questions, and I believe your spirit longs for freedom."

The words she used—so high compared to the words I was accustomed to on the streets. So beautiful, like butterfly wings. I feared touching them and finding them fragile.

"It would mean you would have to agree to keep our secrets." Her tone was like a mother's, and I had to look away. "It would also mean you would leave your place on the streets, and any . . . anything you were doing there to get by."

I knew what she meant. Thank God I did not have *that* to leave behind.

Thank God? Why had I thought that? Were these people affecting me already?

Did I want that? Did I want to stay, to be changed?

Did I want, as Rahab put it, to be free?

twenty-eight
Moving In

If I did move to the compound, it would be nothing more than a decision. I had nothing of value, nothing I needed to go back to my street and retrieve. Everything I owned I was wearing, and considering how long I had worn it without a bath, it was not much to look at either.

Rahab brought me back into the building, where she announced she wanted the women to consider inviting me to stay, along with the newly rescued girl.

The women congregated like a small herd, and I caught a few comments about where I would live, considering all the safe houses would be full if they took the new girl in at the Scarlet Cord.

"Well, we certainly can't send her back to the streets. She's quite pretty, and you know it won't be long before a predator will find her."

Were they talking about me? I felt a twinge of pleasure at being thought pretty, replaced quickly by dread at the thought of being prey. I already had to keep moving regularly to avoid being snatched up during the night while I slept. It was my daily vocation to find a safe place to spend the night.

"Do you think she could stay with Eleanor?"

I looked to see Asha shaking her head. "I know Grandmother would love to have her, but she is weakening these days, and we've actually been talking about asking her to come live with us. I'm concerned about her being here alone when the missionaries are out in the villages."

"Well, we're stuck then, aren't we?"

My head dropped low, but I told myself I was not disappointed. It wasn't like I had even decided I wanted to stay.

"No," Asha said, and my head and my heart lifted with that one word. "I think I might have an idea, but I need to check with Mark first."

I switched my weight from one foot to the other while I looked shyly at the girl in red, who somehow looked even more uncomfortable than I felt.

Milo and Dapika still sat across the room. I saw Dapika sigh; then she surprised me by standing and coming to the girl's side. "Come with me," she said, her voice slow, as if she were still deciding whether or not to say the words. "You . . . too." She motioned toward me, and my eyebrows rose. What was she up to?

She sighed again, then looked back at Milo, who grinned and nodded as if in encouragement. Turning back to us, I saw the tiniest almost-smile. "When I was rescued, someone let me come to their room and get cleaned up, and they gave me clean clothes to wear. I know that's what I'm supposed to do for you, so . . . follow me."

The new girl looked at me questioningly. I shrugged. "Clean sounds good," I said. She let out a nervous giggle, then slapped her hand against her mouth and looked around, as if afraid someone was going to ~~hit her~~ punish her.

My stomach rolled. I remembered that feeling, that fear to have any word or sound or even thought of your own. The haunting knowledge that I could be punished for anything, for nothing, and that the best way to survive was to be as invisible as possible.

With little hesitation, I walked over to stand at the girl's side and put a friendly arm through hers. "You can go first." I felt a real smile emerge on my face. It felt like a long-lost friend.

"I don't know." Milo was grinning. He looked with pride to Dapika, who seemed to glow with the approval, then looked mischievously at me. "You look the dirtiest to me."

A full grin spread my cheeks so far they ached. "Then it's a good thing nobody asked you."

His laughter followed us as we left the room, three random girls thrown together by some unfathomable twist of fate.

Or perhaps, as the women inside would probably say, by the hand of God?

Dear Samir,

Finally, my story has arrived at the present time. Auntie Asha called her husband while I was enjoying my first real bath in months, and by the time I was cleaned up and wearing an outfit from something called a guest closet, she was waiting to invite me to come live in their home for a while. She did not say how long, and I dare not ask. I wake up every day wondering whether today will be the day they tell me to leave, and I have to go back to my life on the streets, but two weeks have passed, and they have not said one word to me about leaving.

Auntie Asha acts like she is happy to have me here, but she is American, so I do not know whether that is true or if she is just acting, as the movie stars do.

Living here is like being in a different ~~village city~~ world. And I do not just mean the foreign food and getting to take a bath every day. There is a difference in the way they talk and the way they act, the things they talk about and how they see the world around them. I do not understand it, but I am drawn to it just as a moth is drawn to light.

Mr. Mark with the yellow hair has given me a Bengali Bible. Every night when I go to bed, I decide to read only a little of it, but I end up staying awake for hours. It is a book unlike any I have ever read—it talks of a God who loves what He made, who forgives even when His people are stubborn and keep making the same mistakes, who makes promises and always keeps them. It is too wonderful to even imagine, but something deep inside me wants Him to be true, to be real. If He is, Samir, He knows us, both of us. Our names. The number of our days in this life. Even the hairs on our head!

As I get ready to go to sleep tonight, it gives me comfort to think that there might be a God who knows where you are, wherever that is, and who is watching over you.

Your sister,
Jasmina

twenty-nine
A Plan

Several days have passed since I last had time to write in this book, but so much has happened I do not know where to start!

Usually the women on the compound do the rescues and then sneak the girls out of the city to the Scarlet Cord or a place called the House of Hope, near Auntie Asha's house, where Auntie and other volunteers help them recover. The trip takes several hours by bus or car, and Auntie Asha says seeing the rice fields and palm trees of the villages helps the girls feel free again.

Sometimes, if there are special rescues planned in the city, Auntie comes and stays with her husband's mother, the woman everyone calls *Grandmother*, for a few days. This time, I begged, and she let me come with her. Of course, she isn't going to let me help with any rescues, but she said I could come with her later to the big street markets to help her stock up on supplies.

Grandmother's house is one of the buildings snug inside the compound wall. Our second afternoon there, I sat with Milo and Dapika, and we have made a plan to rescue the baby!

It is risky, and maybe even a little silly, so we have agreed to keep it a secret just in case it does not work.

I feel the secret bubbling inside me, like soup over a fire, but though I long to tell Asha everything, I fear she would say it is too dangerous and we must not do it.

It is puzzling how you can live in danger for so long, but as soon as safety wraps around you like a comforting blanket, the idea of facing danger again seems so much more . . . dangerous. Not to me, but I know it would to her, so I keep quiet. Though I fear the secret plan will come bursting out my mouth if I am not careful.

But I'm getting ahead of myself . . .

thirty
My Parents

As much as I would wish to skip this part of my story, I know I must write about the day we went to find my parents in our home by the sea. Sometimes I am able to forget they are ~~gone~~ missing, just as my brother is and, I suppose, I am in a way. We are all missing from each other.

The question that beats upon me most, though, is whether they are somewhere missing me.

The day after I came to live with Auntie Asha and Mr. Mark, she sat me down and asked me about a hundred questions until I had told her everything about my life there was to tell, even things I did not think were interesting at all. Like what we ate and how often we ate. Where we bathed. Where we used the bathroom. Who wants to know things like that?

Auntie says that because she grew up in America, there is still much she does not know about real life in India. I guess she thinks my life is "real life," so she wants to know where "real-life" people go to the bathroom.

Because this is of no interest to me at all, I started asking her the same questions about her life in America. She told me about American bathrooms. Americans are very odd. Who would ever think of making a toilet you sit on? And they take things called showers, where the water comes down like a waterfall and washes the dirt off them. Auntie told me they actually have both here in this house! Someday I plan to get up the courage to try the shower. And I want to see the crazy toilet that they sit on, but I do not want to try it. What if I fell in and could not get back out?

After Auntie asked me all about the daily things of our lives, she started asking me about my family. How my father treated my mother. How I was treated, and whether things were different for me than for my brother. The old feelings of bitterness came rushing back, just like the sea when the tide comes in. They swept over me, and for a while I would not talk at all.

Then I looked up and saw that Asha was crying. Not sobbing, just silent tears slipping down her cheeks. She was crying for me.

Somehow, like the shower waterfall, those tears seemed to wash away the hurt I felt at never being as ~~important~~ ~~valued~~ loved.

Asha says God loves girls as much as boys. So there, Samir!

She says God wants husbands to love their wives and fathers to love their children, both the sons and the daughters. Even if I never believe in this God myself, I want to someday marry a man who does. A man who follows this God would be more wonderful than I could imagine.

No, that is not true. I have seen Mr. Mark, and he is a man who loves God and follows Him. He loves his wife, and if he had a child, I know he would love his child no matter what gender it was.

In fact, I believe Mr. Mark and Auntie Asha want a child very much. Their eyes became sad when I asked why they have not had children yet. They have been married three years already. Asha says God has not blessed them with any yet, but His timing is perfect.

When Asha asked, I told her where we lived and that I used to think I needed to find my parents to warn them about the garment factory owner punishing them because we ran away. I did not tell her about how my heart had hardened, and I had decided I did not care. When I spoke of them, I began to care again, and a worry took root deep inside me and began to grow into real fear that they might still be in danger.

As the seed of fear grew, along with it grew a flower of hope. What if Samir had somehow escaped the quarry and gone home? What if my whole family was together except me and they were missing me and longing for me to come back?

I shared this hope with Auntie Asha, and her eyes filled again. I could see she did not hope as I did. She has probably seen too many girls like me, hoping their fathers regretted selling them, only to find such hope as weightless as a cloud, blown away by the slightest breeze.

Seeing her face, knowing the truth of my childhood, I said admitted I did not want to find my home, my parents. I would rather live with this false hope than to know for certain I am still not wanted accepted.

She surprised me by leaving the room. When I found her again, she had a map spread out on the table in the kitchen and was finding the best way to get to my little bamboo shack near the ocean.

"It will be a long trip from here."

"I will work to pay off the debt," I heard myself say. My shoulders immediately felt weighted down with the burden.

"You are not a slave anymore," she said, coming to me and putting a hand on each of my heavy shoulders. "You are free. Do not speak of yourself as a slave, and do not even think about yourself as a slave." She smiled down at me, and I think some of her strength flowed down through her. "God says you are valuable, worth dying for. He loves you, and you matter. Don't ever forget that."

She went back to looking at the map again, but when she noticed me still standing there, she looked up and grinned,

"Besides, I've been wanting to take a trip to the beach for ages. I can't wait to tell Mark!"

thirty-one
The Sea Took My Home

It was gone. Everything. The bamboo that made up the walls. The thatch that was our roof. Even the land beneath our home had been taken out to sea. In its place were huge concrete blocks. To help stop erosion, Mr. Mark said. Why hadn't someone thought to put those there before my world got washed away?

Auntie Asha started asking people questions, but after two or three, I could not bear to hear any more people saying they figured my parents had been washed away in the cyclone along with so many others.

"I might have a little more information," I overheard one person say, "for a price."

Disgusted, my stomach churning, I turned away, pulling Asha with me.

"Don't you want to know whether he knows anything?" Asha asked.

"I want to leave this place," I said firmly. Mr. Mark had seen my face and was already opening the car door for us to get in. "I don't want to hear my own former neighbors making up stories for a little extra money."

My hopes of meeting my parents again, of seeing their faces when they saw me after all these years, disappeared just as my home had. There would be no welcome from my mother. No apology from my father for letting us go.

I was truly alone now.

A cloud of despair followed me into the car and wrapped around my heart as I sat. What would I do now? Should I even bother looking for my brother? Would that search end in disappointment too?

Mr. Mark was driving, and Asha had taken a place in the back seat beside me. She put an arm around my shoulder, and I fought the urge to lean against her and cry like a child.

I sniffed, telling myself that tears were a waste. I was on my own and needed to start acting like it.

"I'm so sorry, Jasmina." Asha's words found their way through the thick fog of my thoughts. "You must feel very lonely right now."

She sighed, and I held my breath, trying to keep the glistening moisture in my eyes from falling out. It worked until she started praying. When she asked God to take care of me and show me He loved me, I could not stop the tears.

Later, I would harden again, be strong, make myself into a shell without feelings so no one could hurt me again. But just for that moment, I let myself be a kid again. I curled up on the seat and lay my head in her lap, and she ran her hand down my hair while she talked. I listened, mostly to the gentle tone of her voice, as she told me how she came to India to work with orphans and accidentally met a trafficked teenage girl. How she foolishly tried to rescue her in her own ignorance and put herself in great danger. And how Mr. Mark had to rescue her.

"More than once," he said from the front seat, looking back quickly with a smile.

"Yes, more than once," she admitted, and I heard love in her voice.

It made the pain in my heart all the more unbearable. They were family, something I no longer had.

As Asha kept talking, she told me about how she decided to spend her life helping rescue trafficked women and children. How trafficking was a problem all over the world, but most people did not know that.

"Surely not in America," I said, sitting up.

"Oh yes, even in America." She looked out the window, as if seeing far away across the ocean to her homeland. "Different methods are used. Instead of lying about free education to parents, as the trafficker did at your home, in America it is often runaway girls who are targeted."

"Why would anyone want to run away? In America, girls have freedom and can make choices. And they are rich. You told me most people have more than one outfit and more than one pair of shoes."

"That's true," she said with a sad smile. "There are places called malls with stores just for clothes or just for shoes."

"A whole store just for shoes?" I could not imagine such ~~wealth~~ ~~luxury~~ extravagance.

"Yes." Her smiled faded. "But even in places like that, there is evil at work. Sometimes a trafficker goes to a place like a mall and offers girls a ride home in his car. Once a girl is in his car, the trafficker steals her away and her freedom is gone."

I thought of my one friend in the garment factory who had been sold by a man who offered her a ride to school. What had happened to her after the fire? Was she safe? Had the boss found her and trafficked her again?

"And Jasmina," Asha touched my hand, "girls in America, however rich or free, can be unhappy and not know their own worth, just like girls here. And if they do not know their worth to God, they start looking for it in other places. Dangerous places. A girl who runs away might meet a man who pretends to love her like her father never did, or who gives her expensive jewelry, or who says he will take care of her. But in time her debt to him grows, and he will expect to be paid. By then it is too late to escape."

I swallowed. Even in America this heavy chain of debt could enslave people, as it had me. I thought about what would likely happen to me if I returned to the streets, and my body filled with cold terror. All my pretended courage, all my assurances to myself that I could handle life out there, that I could protect myself, evaporated. Right then, somehow, I saw clearly the direction I was headed. How had I ever convinced myself that I could live safe and free out there on the streets?

Suddenly desperate, I clutched at Asha's arm. "I don't want to go back to the streets," I said, pleading for my life. "I know what will happen to me. I don't want to live my life in a brothel, never allowed outside, never seeing the light, belonging to everyone but myself. Please, please let me stay in a safe house or with you. I'll work hard. I'll be your slave. Just don't send me back to the streets."

"Oh, Jasmina." Her voice was full of pain, and I curled up on the seat, bracing myself for another rejection. "I had no idea you thought—we would never send you back out there! You are welcome with us or in the safe houses for as long as you want to stay." Her smile was a gift. "I didn't say anything earlier in the hopes that your parents would want you back. Now that . . . well, just know that you have a place among us. We value you and want you to be safe."

Safe. What a powerful word. I had never been able to hold that word to my heart before, but now, very cautiously, I took it and clutched it tightly.

"Jasmina, the Bible has a verse that says, 'When my father and my mother forsake me, then the Lord will take care of me.' God has a very big family, and He wants you to be part of it. Until then, though, you can be part of ours."

thirty-two
The Plan to Save the Baby

"I don't know whether this will work." Dapika skeptically held up the can of shaving cream. "If it doesn't, we are going to be in so much trouble."

I thought of Auntie Asha saying she tried to rescue a girl in ignorance and Mr. Mark had to come rescue her. Was that what we were doing, acting in ignorance? I thought of Milo coming to rescue me but brushed that idea away. He was part of the plan, after all.

"It's worth a try." Milo's grin never left his face. "Besides, I've always wanted to try this, just to play a joke on someone. But I decided it was a mean joke, so I never did. Now I'll get to!"

His excitement was contagious. It swished inside me, all mixed up with my worry and my own doubts that this was way too far-fetched an idea to actually work. "Well, Asha said we are leaving the compound tomorrow, so we have only today. Are we ready to do this?"

"Sure."

"No."

I looked from Milo's confident smile to Dapika's scowl. "We won't be back for weeks. Do you really want to wait that long to try to save that baby?"

"Come on; let's just go. We're not going to come up with any better ideas later. The ladies around here have been trying for weeks and haven't come up with anything at all." Milo grinned again. "My idea may be silly, but it's the only one we've got."

Dapika bit her lip. "But what if it doesn't work? We could all end up caught and trafficked ourselves."

"No way." Milo's voice took on a sternness I had not heard before. "I would never let anyone take you away."

Dapika blushed, and I felt envy rise up within me at how Milo looked at her so ~~tenderly~~ protectively. "I've been part of rescue missions before," he said. "We did something a little like this once when we had to get across a bridge." His grin was back. "I'm very good at causing a disturbance."

My insides were all knotting up. "Okay, let's go. If we stay here any longer, I'll lose my nerve."

I watched Dapika look to Milo. Still biting her lip, she nodded. "Okay."

They exited the room and I heard Milo calling for the stray dog that lived just outside the compound. Several weeks ago Milo had found it scavenging for food nearby, and he had decided it would be his personal pet. Feeding it scraps from his meals had made the dog into a fast friend.

I hesitated and then on impulse found a scrap of paper and wrote a small note. I could not venture back out onto the streets on such a dangerous mission—however silly our method might be—without leaving some word. I knew too well how quickly things could go wrong. Milo used to live on the streets, but he seemed to have forgotten some of its dangers. I had not.

After signing my name at the bottom, I put the pencil across the paper to weigh it down, hoping no one would find it too soon.

Or too late.

thirty-three
The Rescue

"We're heading out for a while." Milo's tone was perfectly casual as he waved to his father, who guarded the gate of the compound. "I'm hungry for a snack and want to get some *pani puri*."

His father waved back as the gate swung shut behind us. We stood there at the edge of the street, looking as ~~young incapable~~ unprepared as I felt.

The stray dog nudged Milo's hand, and he laughed. "Come along, Hero." He looked at me. "That's what I've named him. We'll see if he earns his name today."

We crossed the street, and Milo bartered with a rickshaw driver. He ended up having to pay extra because the driver had no desire to transport the mangy dog along with all of us. Milo, however, won in the end. I wondered whether anyone had ever refused him anything. He had a knack for getting people to see things his way.

I only hoped his confidence and quick thinking would help us succeed today.

"We should pray."

I looked over at Milo with surprise. I did not have to look far—we were all squeezed quite tightly onto the one rickshaw seat, the dog wagging his tail from his perch in front of our feet. "Pray?"

"Of course." Milo grinned at me. "I may have a great plan, but it's no good at all without God's help. God is the one we need to ask to help us rescue that baby."

He bowed his head, and Dapika did as well. I stared as he asked God for protection for us and freedom for the baby. I could not imagine my brother doing such a thing, humbling himself so. But instead of lowering Milo in my eyes, the action filled me respect for him. What would it be like to have a family who followed God like this always? What would it be like to have a husband who called on God, who—

I stopped myself from those thoughts. I had no intention of ever having a husband. I had not escaped being a slave for one man to become a servant for another and—

"We're here. This is the road near the district bridge."

Glad for the distraction in my thoughts, I climbed down from the rickshaw after Milo, Dapika, and the dog. Milo took the shaving cream from his pocket and shook the container. We walked a block, then turned into an alley. From there we could see the bridge, the courtyard, and the baby. She was still tied to a pole with that red rope. Had Rahab been right? Did that red rope symbolize freedom and deliverance?

I sure hoped so, or we were all going to lose our freedom by the end of the day.

"Remember what to do?"

Milo was looking at Dapika, who nodded. He looked at me. I nodded.

We all took in a deep breath. "Okay, then. Let's go."

Starting with a soft tread, we sneaked out of the alley and down the street, stopping to hide behind a small peddler's cart. Milo once again shook up the can of shaving cream. "You're first," he said to me.

His smile, full of faith, was the only thing that moved me forward. I had no confidence in my acting ability, but Milo must have known I would be more convincing than Dapika at least. I approached the man guarding the bridge to the district. "I need to talk to the madam," I said, trying to insert authority into my voice.

"Which madam?"

Which madam? Oh no, I had not thought of that! Of course, there would be more than one. "The—the one who owns that baby right there." I nodded my chin toward the baby. The man frowned.

This already wasn't going so well. Were we doomed to failure before we even started?

thirty-four
Bluffing

The man did not leave his post to find the madam, so I had to swallow that hope. If he had, we could have just run across the bridge, grabbed the baby, untied her, and run back.

As that was obviously not going to be an option, we would have to stick to Milo's plan, one that seemed more ridiculous by the second.

Summoning another man to go into the maze of buildings, the guard stood leering at me, his eyes going up and down my body in a way that made me break out in a cold sweat.

"You looking for a job, sweet thing?" His mouth tipped upward, and I fought the urge to gag. A wave of nausea and disgust—that I was almost sold into this life—swept over me. Just as I was about to turn and flee, an ancient woman emerged from one of the rooms and sauntered across the courtyard. Her hair was teased into a ball around her head, and she wore at least three layers of makeup, none of which hid the wrinkles overtaking her features.

I unconsciously took a step back as the woman approached the bridge where I stood. Her cheap perfume smelled as gaudy as the fake jewelry she wore. I tried to keep my face passive while she looked me over the same way I would look over a piece of fruit in the market.

"Whaddayawant?" The woman's words slurred together. She was either drunk or on some kind of drug. That could work to my advantage.

"I—I want to buy that baby," I said, putting my shoulders back and hoping I looked older than my years.

The madam looked back at the child tied to the pole. The baby whimpered, and I felt my heart breaking at the fear I saw in her eyes. Now, without a doubt, I knew who her bruises had come from.

"What for?" the woman barked.

"I know a family who wants to adopt a baby."

"Families want to adopt boyeez." Her words stretched out and were hard to understand. "Don't be stu-u-u-pid."

"Not this one. They just want a baby, even a girl." I thought of Auntie Asha and Mr. Mark. Yes, they wanted a baby more than anything. I knew it from watching them. What would they think if I were to carry this baby to them and hand her over?

"How much?"

I shook my head, annoyed at myself for getting distracted. "First let me see her. I want to make sure she isn't damaged. You shouldn't keep her out here in the sun if you want to sell her."

"You can see the ba-a-a-ybee when I see the mu-u-u-nee."

I forced myself to take in a breath, then let it out. I had no money. With an inward cry for help to someone, maybe to Asha's God, I said, "Do you really think I'm foolish enough to bring the money with me and get pickpocketed by one of your little beggars? The money is in a safe place, and you won't see it until after I see that baby."

The madam swayed as she took a step. She grunted at my words but motioned for the guard to let me pass. I put a hand to my chest so she wouldn't notice my shawl bouncing away from my pounding heart. Stepping quickly across the bridge, I headed for the child, stopping when she cried out in fear.

"Don't worry, sweetie," I said softly. "It's okay."

When the madam came closer to me, her half-lidded eyes full of suspicion, I realized my error too late. I should not have spoken gently to this child. I should act like I don't care.

"What are you reel-ly doing here?" the woman asked, her voice still slurred but very aware. My insides were shaking. Where was Milo?

Oh, I hadn't given him the signal!

thirty-five
Hero to the Rescue

"Want something yummy?" I held out a portion of a cookie to the baby. *Please take it, please take it.* The baby reached out—

Suddenly a barking dog came charging toward the guard at the gate. He cursed and abandoned his post. "Rabid dog! Mad dog!" he shouted as he ran.

The madam stopped staring me down and looked toward the bridge. She shrieked and backed away.

I did too, trying not to laugh at Hero bounding toward us with shaving cream all over his mouth. The dog ran straight to the baby, or rather straight to the cookie just like the ones Milo had been feeding him for days. The baby had put the cookie to her little mouth, and the dog slobbered all over her face in attempt to get his share.

"Aagh!" the madam screamed. "Get that mad dog away! Away!"

If there had been any chance the dog might, indeed, have rabies, I would have been running myself. Rabies is deadly. Shaving cream, however, is not, so I stayed close enough to make sure the dog didn't get too carried away as he made friends with the baby. She helped our plan immensely by crying in fierce wails. I'm sure it was in anger that the dog had eaten half her cookie, but the madam saw the reaction differently.

"He bit her! He bit her! She'll get rabies! Get her out of here!"

Milo came running, or at least hurrying with his crutch, up to the edge of the bridge. "I can help you!" he shouted. He held another cookie over his head. "Hey, dog, come and get it!"

Hero enthusiastically followed the plan, bounding toward his master and the cookie, his tail flapping side to side at the fun game. I knew Dapika was farther down the road, ready for our getaway.

I looked at the baby, who now had Hero's shaving cream all over her face, then looked up at the madam. She was hiding most of her body around the corner, screaming at the top of her lungs for someone to get the dog and the baby away from her before they all died or went mad.

Rather dramatic, but not too surprising if she were on some sort of hallucinogen. I had seen a few people on the streets try those drugs, and they would go temporarily insane, seeing all sorts of terrible things and moaning or yelling.

My fingers clumsily yanked at the red cord securing the baby to the pole. It held fast. How long had she been tied up here?

"Take her away! Take her away!"

A knife clattered across the courtyard; the madam must have slipped it from her position of safety. I grabbed it and quickly cut the cord where it knotted around the pole. I picked up the baby, who continued crying, the red rope dangling from her bruised ankle.

"You're saying I can have this baby, right?" I'm not sure why I felt the need to double check. I suppose because I didn't want her sending someone after me later. "What about the money?"

"The money." The woman's eyes turned shrewd and she held out her hand. "Give me the money."

"I told you I don't have it. Do you want me to go get it?" I stepped closer to her, being sure to hold the baby in front of me so the madam could see the shaving cream.

"Just get away! Take her away! I don't care!"

I could not keep from grinning. "Thanks very much!" I called out, turning on my heel and running across the bridge.

The bouncing motion got the baby's attention. She stopped crying and looked around with big, curious eyes.

"Hello, Baby," I said with a smile. "Guess what? You just got freed."

thirty-six
In Trouble

The baby stared at me blankly, and I laughed as I ran to catch up to Milo. Around the corner, Dapika would be waiting with the rickshaw, and we could all go ~~home~~ back to the compound.

Once in the rickshaw, Hero barking his delight, I used my shawl to wipe the shaving cream from the baby's face. Even Dapika's perpetual scowl had melted at the sight of the child. "You're on your way to meet your new parents," I said softly as I finished cleaning the baby up. She gurgled and flailed her arms.

Milo laughed at the baby's toothy grin but then looked at me with questions in his eyes. "You mentioned parents. Do you have a family for the baby?" He chuckled. "Or are you planning to get married and keep her yourself?"

For one second a scene flashed through my mind—me holding a baby, a husband cradling us both in his arms. An impossible scene of love.

No. I shook my head. "I am taking the baby to ones who will love her" was all I said.

Milo started to ask another question, but we had arrived at the compound gate. Milo's father was already in the process of opening it. How did he know we were coming right then? The gate swung open wide and then I saw it. A familiar Land Rover. Mr. Mark behind the wheel. Asha in the passenger seat.

Eyes wide, our rickshaw driver began to pedal away from the giant vehicle's path, but I yelled, "Stop!" I clambered over the dog and down from the rickshaw just as doors opened from both sides of the Land Rover and both Asha and Mr. Mark ~~burst~~ ~~jumped~~ fell out.

"Uh-oh." I moved toward them even as my heart sank. Asha's eyes were blazing and not with happiness. When her gaze dropped to the baby in my arms, her face paled and for a moment, a light of hope shined bright. Then fear took its place.

"What on earth have you done?" Her eyes went from me to Dapika to Milo. "You three scared me half to death! We were just headed toward the district to look for you!"

"How did you know we were going to the district?" Milo and Dapika had both climbed down from the rickshaw and stood behind me, leaving me in front to take the blame.

I pursed my lips and looked back at him. "I left a note, just in case."

"You left a note?"

"Well, what if we'd been kidnapped or something? Wouldn't you want somebody to know where we went?"

Dapika stepped forward. "That was a good idea," she said. I felt vindicated and smiled at her, but when I looked back at Asha, my smile fell.

"What is going on here?" she asked. "And what are you doing with that baby?"

thirty-seven
God's Treasure

Milo, Dapika, and I sat on the couch back in the building where I had left the note. Hero had been sent outside the gate, with a few cookies as reward. Auntie Asha paced in front of us while Mr. Mark parked the Land Rover. Every once in a while, Asha would gravitate over to the baby bouncing on my knee, but then she would pull back and start her pacing again, muttering to herself.

The moment Mr. Mark opened the door, she started in on us. "How could you do a thing like this? Don't you know how dangerous it is to go into that area? What were you thinking?"

All the tension that had built up in me came pouring out. "I was thinking that you and Mr. Mark wanted a baby!" I shouted. The child in my arms jerked at the sound and turned to look at me. I stood and balanced her on my hip. "I was thinking that everybody wanted to rescue this baby but nobody could think of a way to do it. Why are you angry with me for succeeding?"

My guilt multiplied tenfold when she started crying. "I was so worried," she said, her voice muffled behind her hands.

Mr. Mark came close. If they had been alone, I know he would have wrapped his arms around her. I had seen him do so before when she was upset. Something inside me sighed.

"Asha, my love." His voice was so soft, I could barely hear him. "They are all safe, and you have to admit, somehow they did succeed." She lifted her wet face, and he grinned down at her. "Now you know how I felt all those times you went running off on your own without telling me."

She looked at me. Tears still glistened in her eyes, but she smiled when her husband behind her said, "She's like you, you know. Full of courage and heart, and maybe a little too much impulsiveness."

His words made my heart sing. I took the two steps that separated us and held the baby out. Asha hesitantly opened her arms, and the baby moved easily into them. I suppose any person, even a stranger, would be preferable to sitting on the hard concrete ground, tied to a pole.

"Oh, you beautiful little girl," Asha murmured. She reached down and touched the red rope still dangling from her ankle. "How did they ever get you free?"

Milo jumped up, glad to tell the story of his success. The more he talked, the more Asha's mouth dropped open. When he got to the part about the shaving cream, Mr. Mark burst out laughing. "Bravo!" he said. I did not know what that word meant, but it must be a good thing because Milo grinned wide.

"I saved the day!" he said when his story was finished. Asha shook her head in wonder as she looked from Milo to the baby. Her heart was in her eyes. She looked up at Mr. Mark. "Do you think a judge would believe that she just gave the baby up? Would we need to . . . well, what would we need to do to keep her?"

"I don't know all the legalities for getting a baby from a place like that," he responded, smiling when the baby gripped one of his fingers with her whole hand. "But I will find out."

"Oh, Mark." She had forgotten the rest of us were in the room. Her head dropped to rest on her husband's shoulder, and her smile went dreamy. "Her name is Adiya. It means 'God's treasure.'" She looked up again. "If that's all right with you, of course."

His smile at her was so full of love it made my heart ache. Would I ever know a love like that? Looking at the three of them, the baby happily sucking her fingers as she nestled between them, the ache spread. If they were allowed to adopt the baby, there would be no more room for someone like me in their lives. I would still be grateful to live at the Scarlet Cord, or one of the other safe houses, but it would not be the same.

I turned away from the happy sight, from the family that could never be mine.

Dear Samir,

I only have two pages left in my book that used to be blank. I wish I had ten. So much has happened since I last wrote to you.

Auntie Asha and Mr. Mark have been busy working to adopt a baby I helped rescue. They're so happy with the baby that I tried to not let my sadness show as I packed up the few things that belonged to me. The toothbrush they gave me that had never even been used before. The pair of sandals Asha said I could have. The Bengali Bible from Mr. Mark . . .

Looking around the room, the first place in my life that had been all my own for a while, I jumped when I heard Auntie say, "Jasmina, could you come here, please?"

I hoped she was going to ask me to help with the baby. Little Adiya has stolen all our hearts. It is impossible not to love her big smiles and glad squeals, even if she is taking my place in this house.

But when I went into the room, Mr. Mark, Auntie Asha, and the baby all stared at me, smiling. Well, baby Adiya wasn't smiling; she was drooling all over the fingers in her mouth. "Did you need me to help with something?"

"Yes and no," Asha said secretively.

I was too sad to play games, so just said, "What is it?"

"We think it is going to be possible for us to adopt the baby," Mr. Mark said. His voice was happy. "We wanted to say thank you for risking so much to get freedom for her—"

"And bringing her to us," Asha finished for him. She held the little girl tightly, as if remembering where she had come from. I looked at the baby's arms. Her bruises were almost gone.

Asha stood and handed Adiya to her husband. Then she came close to me and put her arms around me. I had never been hugged before. I did not know what to do.

"Thank you," she whispered, tears in her eyes. "She is a gift from God."

I nodded.

"And so are you."

Me? I looked into eyes that were full of love—love for me. I thought that love was only for the baby.

"Jasmina, would you stay with us? We can't adopt you. We do not know whether your parents are still living. But we would love to have you as part of our family. You could be like my little sister. And you could help with the baby sometimes, if you want."

I could not speak. I would have a real home, a real family?

Asha took a step back as she looked at my face. "You don't have to, of course. You could live in one of the safe houses, or—"

"Oh, I want to!" I was breathless with joy. "I want to more than anything!"

She pulled me into a hug again, and this time I threw my arms around her.

Oh, Samir, how my life has changed since the last day I saw you! You watched me be taken away to a lifetime of slavery, but now here I am, free, in a home full of love. Auntie Asha—or rather Didi, since she is my big sister now—has plans for me to help with the baby, but I have bigger plans. I am going to help her rescue other girls like me. I will help her give them hope again.

I will keep looking for you, Samir. I will even ask God to help me find you, though I am not sure I believe in Him yet.

Someday we will sit together and I will tell you about all I have written. Of Milo and Dapika and the women at the Scarlet Cord. Of a dog who is a hero. Of a red rope that now hangs limp and useless on a wall in ~~Auntie Asha's~~ my house.

Mostly, I will tell you of a slave who is free, a girl who used to be alone and afraid but is now looking at the future with hope.

Your sister always,
Jasmina